RULE HIM

FORBIDDEN FANTASIES: BOOK ONE.

ANGEL DEVLIN

ALL RIGHTS RESERVED.
No part of this publication may be reproduced, distributed, or transmitted in any form or by any means, including photocopying, recording, or other electronic or mechanical methods, without the prior written permission of the publisher, with the exception of the use of small quotations in book reviews.
Copyright © 2018 By Angel Devlin.
Second edition © Angel Devlin, 2022.

Cover Design by The Pretty Little Design Company
Formatting by Angel Devlin.

This is a work of fiction. Any resemblance of characters to actual persons, living or dead, is purely coincidental. Angel Devlin holds exclusive rights to this work. Unauthorized duplication is prohibited.

1

CANDY

"You have to lose the V-card this semester," ordered my best friend, Larissa.

It was fine for her; she'd been in love with Jeff Williams since eighth grade. They had gotten engaged a couple of months ago, and she had their whole future life mapped out. Exactly when they would get married, how many kids they would have, where they would live after college. It helped that both of them, like me, were from the Upper East Side in New York City with parents who had so much wealth we didn't discuss it. Most around here flaunted it instead: 'Oh look what Daddy got me when he returned from Singapore,' then they would show off their latest vintage Rolex. Everything had to be the latest trend. Every step was one-upmanship. In truth, deep inside I found it all dull, but if I didn't go along with it, I'd be the laughing stock of

Lincoln High and no one ever wanted to make themselves that. So instead I immersed myself in the latest fashions, talked about boys, and right now, planned for my eighteenth birthday party, which was to be *the* party of the year according to my mom. My father was in politics, and my mom ran her own interior design biz. I didn't see them much, usually only when they needed to show me off to their guests at a soiree. That was fine with me. When my best friend had gone home, I liked my own company. I loved anything involving words and using my brain: reading, watching the news, etc. Right now, my brain was screaming for me to make Larissa go home.

"I'm not rushing to lose my virginity. I want to be in love. It's important to me," I replied, as I rubbed my brow.

"Oh, you can always pretend on your wedding night. Just say your battery operated boyfriend broke your hymen." Larissa waved off my response.

"No." I became so pissed by this point I snapped the pencil I was holding in half. Larissa either failed to notice or ignored me. Either way, she didn't give up.

"Julian Murphy likes you. He's hot."

Julian was the star player of the varsity baseball team. He was the guy all the girls wanted; even loved-up Larissa found him 'to die for.' He did nothing for me. He was good looking, sure. All tall and lean with a fit body and a perfect smile. But he lived for sports, and I loathed them. Plus, he liked to collect girls' V-cards like trophies, so there was that. I was not going to be a notch on a bedpost.

No, I dreamed of my perfect guy. He would be hugely intelligent. Tall. Dark-haired. Maybe of slim build, rather than pumped up muscles. Gentle and kind. He'd look at me like I was his everything. Larissa said I read too many fairy tales when I was growing up. Huh, our lives were like fairy tales: balls, designer gowns and shoes, staff to do our bidding. Maybe what I wanted was an anti-fairy tale, where I was the princess who went after the prince, not the other way around.

"Earth calling Candy."

"Huh?"

"You went off in a daydream again there, Candy. Now, your eighteenth. What's going to be the theme?"

"Sleeping Beauty," I announced.

"What? That movie's been out for months now. Sleeping Beauty is over. You need something different, girl."

"I want to do Sleeping Beauty," I insisted. For presents I want books. I'm going to build a huge library like the one the Beast had. Mom said for my birthday I could have the guest room next to mine. She's going to have an adjoining door put in, so it will be perfect."

Larissa's brow creased. "Your mom is okay with you having a library room?"

I sighed. "Not exactly; it's supposed to be an even larger walk-in closet. One with luxury seating where she can get designers to visit me in person, rather than using her room."

"Good luck with that then, honey. Anyhow, I'm with your mom on this one. Books? Forget books, collect shoes!"

Larissa looked at her Givenchy watch, her blonde carefully streaked and blown out long tresses fell forward as she bent her head. "Oh crap, I should have called a driver by now. I'd arranged to meet Jeff at six." She grabbed her purse and jacket and kissed me on both cheeks before running to the door.

"Laters, baby," she giggled. Fifty Shades had recently released on DVD, and she kept telling me she and Jeff were using it as inspiration. Far too much information.

With that, my bedroom door closed and I was left alone in peace.

My room was my haven. A large space with light wooden floors with underfloor heating; my bed sat atop a large Madeline Weinrib rug. Vast curtains hung from three high windows and as well as my current walk-in closet; I had two purple velvet armchairs and a chaise longue. These were beside a wall of bookcases, filled to the brim with novels and non-fiction. I had a thirst for knowledge and an overwhelming urge to break free from my gilded cage to explore the world out there. Just Manhattan itself held untold secrets. I'd never visited places like Carlo's Bake Shop. My mom would say, 'What's the need when our staff could make you your own pignoli cookies?'

I was relieved to be back in school tomorrow. As it was my last semester, I needed to study hard. My dream was to write novels, but my teachers held the belief I would work for my mom's company after graduation. I could if I wanted; I was on course to pass art. It would seem I'd gained this talent genetically, but my head and heart yearned to write novels like the one's I read voraciously. The only time I'd mentioned this to my mom she had rolled her eyes. It hadn't even been worthy of a comment. I wanted to train as an English teacher so that I could hopefully instill the same love for prose as I had, in other student's lives, and then write in my spare time. My mom would accuse me of trying to make her a laughingstock, which was why I hadn't told her my plans. I was doing extra classes to earn credits for college, and I needed some additional tutoring to ensure my grades were the best they could be. I was looking forward to the morning when I could get out of the townhouse and get back to my studies, and see if there were any teachers or students offering mentoring or tutoring this final semester.

I grabbed a romance book from my nightstand and picked up where I'd left off. For all my romantic dreams, and hearts, flowers and fairy tale ideas, I liked a bedtime read that gave me an idea of what I might expect once I did find a man to take me to bed. I loved to read in detail about tongues trailing down warm flesh, lips nibbling, fingers delving into warm, wet places. On the rare occasions I masturbated, I always felt ashamed afterwards, like I was doing something bad. Another prison I was captured in, this time in my mind. Turning to where I'd left off reading last time, I continued to read on, my mind making me the heroine in the book while doing my best to avoid noticing the dampness from my core which was soaking into my panties.

The day was underway at Lincoln High, and it seemed as if we'd had no break at all. I slipped back into my routine like it was a comfy pair of slippers. My first class after lunch was English. I knew we had a new teacher as our previous one, Mrs. Donovan, had left to have a baby and wasn't coming back. It was annoying to change teachers at this stage in our education. I wanted to study as much English as I could and worried that if I didn't like the new teacher, it might affect my grades. Larissa started gossiping to me about something or other she'd heard on campus so I heard the door open but I didn't see who came through it.

I guess I should have known by the fact that the entire female population of the class went silent, that a hot male had walked through the door before I turned around.

But when I did, *holy hell!*

A gray jacket, gray pants, and a crisp, white shirt encased the body of a god. He was lean but athletic. As he moved to place his laptop case on the desk at the front of the classroom, his jacket gaped open showing the shirt stretched against his chest. You could make out his pecs, and I knew just from that brief look that he worked out, whether it was via a gym he visited or regular sports he played. His light brown hair was short but sculpted with paste. I didn't fail to notice that he was built like the heroes of my romance novels. I felt my body warm up by a billion degrees and I swept my bangs out of my face to try to cool myself down a little.

"Holy crap, he's gorgeous. I'm up for studying if the subject is the teacher," Larissa whispered directly into my ear.

"Sshh," I warned her. She was in danger of being a little too loud.

The god-like creature spoke.

"Hey there. I'm Mr. Newell, and I'm your new English teacher."

His voice was deep and husky. He should have been paid to narrate commercials, not be stuck in high school with a bunch of awkward teenagers.

It was a few minutes later when Larissa prodded me in the arm.

"Hey, what's that for?" I asked her.

"She's called Candy," Larissa said.

"Candy." Mr. Newell looked at his register. "Ah yes, Candy Appleton. Candy, we were just all introducing ourselves so I could get to know you a little, so if you're not too busy daydreaming, perhaps you could tell me a bit about yourself?"

I flushed what must have been a deep shade of pink. I'd been so busy mooning over the hot, new teacher and thinking about him in a scene from the book I'd read last night that I'd had no clue he had carried on addressing the class and started introductions. Disappearing into a world of my imagination was a bad habit of mine. When I'd been younger, I'd been known to be so engrossed in books that I hadn't had a clue as to what was happening in my current surroundings. Larissa once left me alone with a book because I had blissed out on words in the school library and I hadn't noticed she had gone until my cell had buzzed thirty minutes later. I was a lost cause to literature, and now it seemed a lost cause to lusting after sexy new male teachers.

"I'm sorry, Mr. Newell. I didn't sleep well, and I must have drifted a little," I lied. "My name is Candy Appleton. Erm, what else did you want to know?"

"Your favorite subject and what you hoped to do after graduation." His lip was in a firm line, and I didn't know if he was upset with me or amused.

"My favorite subject is English. I love literature, and I hope to become an English teacher." I told him truthfully, hoping he didn't think I was making it up in order to appease him for my daydreaming.

"Well, in that case, maybe you need to make sure you get enough sleep for future lessons so you can achieve your dreams," he replied, and then he moved on to the next student.

I felt like he'd physically slapped me. I was a great student with no problems in English, and before today I didn't remember ever being scolded by a teacher. Larissa was the one who got pulled up in lessons as she continually sneaked peeks at her cell to see if Jeff had messaged her.

For the rest of the class, I made sure to keep my head down. I listened to what he said to the class, but I tried to avoid eye contact with him. If I thought he was about to look my way, or if he did, I quickly averted my gaze. Great. My favorite lesson was now going to become the one I dreaded most. Then I almost physically groaned. I needed to speak to him after class to see if he knew of anyone who could give me extra tutoring when all I wanted was to bolt from the classroom.

The bell sounded, and everyone packed their belongings away and began to leave. I hovered around Mr. Newell's desk as another three female students had got there first. They were asking ridiculous questions, and I knew they were doing it just to try to get his attention. I could see Brandy Elliott side-eyeing me as if to tell me to get lost.

Finally, they left, and it was just him and me.

"Miss Appleton. How can I help you?" He tilted his head to the side.

In class, the teachers called us by our first names, so I felt I was being reprimanded once again with the formal use of my last name.

"I'm looking for some extra tutoring this term to improve my grades for college. I wondered if you knew anyone? I appreciate you just got here and so you might not have any information for me right now, but I would be grateful if you could look into it for me. Mainly, I'd like to focus some more on film and literature."

"Right. Anything in particular? The romantic poets like Wordsworth and Keats for example?"

I looked up at him for the first proper time all lesson. His face bore no hint of a smile or the friendliness with which he'd addressed the class. Rather, he looked irritated.

"I'd like to look at developing screenplays in particular and anything about character development. I'm hoping to write a novel someday." It was the first time I'd voiced that out loud to anyone, but this man's acerbic manner had got to me. What had I done to warrant it? I'd only daydreamed a little in class.

He rubbed his forehead.

"I'm sorry," he said. "It's just I get that a lot. Female students asking for extra tutoring when they want me to quote romantic love poems to them really and have no interest in learning at all. Take a seat, Candy; it would appear we got off on the wrong foot, so let's start again. Now, what's this about writing your own novel? What are you interested in writing about?"

Though I was annoyed that he thought I wanted him to read love poems to me, I considered the girls who had stood there before me and the fact I'd daydreamed about him, and decided to move on. I pulled up a chair at the side of his desk, and he sat back down himself.

"I have a jotter at home, and I write in it often. Lots

of character observations and things I find witty or interesting. I'd like to write a novel about someone who's trapped in life and wants to spread their wings. I don't have any more details at the moment. It's just been a dream. I never told anyone before. I always say I want to be an English teacher."

"So, you don't?" he asked.

I shrugged. "I think I'd be a good teacher, but my mom is an interior designer and is set on me working for her."

His face got the look everyone's got when they realized who my mom was.

"You're Irena Appleton's daughter?"

I sighed. "Yes."

"Ah." He studied my face. "And you don't share the same ambition, I take it?"

"I appreciate what my mom does, and her talent is out of this world. I'm good at art. There's no reason why I shouldn't go into the business..."

"Except your heart is in English?"

"You got it, and if writing a novel is too ambitious—and I'm not stupid, I know my chances of getting a traditional deal are like identifying an individual raindrop in a puddle—then being a teacher of English would be my next dream, so I can try to get other people to see how beautiful the language is."

"Candy, you know that as a teacher, mainly you

just try to get through class without students breaking out in a fight? If they open the textbook in a lesson, you think you've done well."

He looked downbeat.

"Surely it's not that bad?"

He shook his head. "It was at my last school. I'm hoping here it's going to be a little different, and seeing as I already have at least one student who loves English, I guess I'm already ahead. I'll tutor you myself. That way, if no one else in the entire school likes English, at least I'll have one student I can bore with literature. Do Mondays and Thursdays straight after school fit in with your schedule?

I thought of my week. All I'd need to do was quit the senior prom committee which would be a bonus as it was another pain in my ass. As Larissa kept reminding me, I needed to get a date for it, and I didn't want one. My mom was also all prom, prom, prom, as if I would be attending a royal ball, not an end of school year party. 'Oh, it's so important. I loved mine with your father,' was all I ever heard about these days; well, that and my eighteenth.

"Those days would be fine. Thank you so much, Mr. Newell, and I'm sorry again, for the daydreaming. I'm an attentive student usually, I promise."

He smiled, revealing a perfect set of white teeth.

His lips had just the correct amount of plumpness and framed his teeth beautifully when he smiled.

I realized I was in danger of daydreaming again, so I jumped up.

"Thanks again, Mr. Newell. I'll see you after school Thursday."

And with that, I dashed from the classroom.

Larissa was hanging around outside. She usually rushed straight off to see Jeff, so she was trying to hit me up for gossip.

"So, what was that all about, Candy? Are you trying to get detention so that you can have him all to yourself?"

I gave her a nudge. "I was asking him about extra tutoring. I already told you I needed it before your new man crush arrived in class."

"You mean you don't find him attractive? Are you completely blind?"

"He's okay, I guess." I giggled.

She looked me up and down. "You can quit that innocent look. I've known you since kindergarten. You are so hot for the teacher."

"Stop it. Be quiet." I hissed, looking back at the door. "He'll hear you."

"I'll be quiet if you admit the truth." She wiggled her eyebrows at me.

"He is freaking gorgeous," I admitted. "Just like the

men in my books. But he's a teacher, and I do want help with my grades, so I asked if he could suggest anyone."

"And did he?"

I nodded. "He's going to tutor me Monday's and Thursday's after school."

"You lucky bitch." Larissa wrapped her arm around me. "After school let's go collect Jeff and head to Bailey's for ice cream. I think we both need to cool down after that lesson."

2

PARKER

This is what I swore would never happen to me. After all the trouble at the private girls' school I'd just left, the last thing I needed was close involvement with a student. Never again did I want accusations about my professional conduct. I'd left Queens with my reputation intact, but my engagement was broken. In some ways, it had done me a favor. I had loved Eliza. I'd known her since we were teenagers—but it wasn't enough. The drama at Elvington High had shown us both facets of each other we hadn't noticed before as we went through the routine of life—mainly that neither of us was in love with the other.

Time had passed. I'd taken six months off to spend some time deciding on what I wanted to do in the future. My father had tried to drag me back into the family business—he ran a multi-million dollar publishing company—but as always, as the 'black sheep' of the family, I'd resisted. Now here I was at Lincoln High, a mixed-sex school where I was hoping for a drama-free life.

I had deliberately decided to work with twelfth graders. They were seventeen and eighteen and so I had figured there would be fewer schoolgirl crushes, the hormones having calmed down by now. Plus as a mixed-sex school, they had plenty of the opposite sex their own age to annoy and hook up with. So when after my class today I'd had nothing but female students hanging around asking dumb ass questions, I'd been at the end of my rope. When Candy had asked about private tutoring, I'd lost it for a moment, believing she was just like the rest of them, wanting time to crush on me, paid for by her no doubt super rich parents.

But she was different—and that was so much worse.

The minute I'd noticed the long-haired brunette with the blow job mouth sitting in my class, I had felt like a lightning bolt had hit me. Throw all the clichés my way. Time stood still. I had felt a connection. It was like somehow I felt I had known her all my life. But I hadn't. She was a student in my English class, and I was there to teach. When we had started the class introductions, I'd noticed that she was staring in my direction—blankly staring—with no idea that it was her turn to introduce herself, and then her friend had prodded her, and she had blushed. Well if that blush hadn't made her whole face look like a china doll's. Just entirely like she was a precious object, and I had felt an extra hard beat of my heart. So I had berated her, pulled her up on her behavior, so I could distract myself and make myself feel better. And then she'd said her name—Candy Appleton. She couldn't have been named any better if her parents had gone with Snow White. She was sweet as Candy, and I did want a bite of that apple. I couldn't wait for class to be over. I needed to get out of there, get to my usual session at the pool and work this insanity from my system.

And then she'd asked for the tutoring.

When it had become clear that she was a lover of the English language and eager to learn, I had not been able to resist. Students who wanted to study hard and have a career in the subject should be encouraged. Plus, the thought of anyone else with one-on-one time with her made my blood boil in my veins. What the hell was happening to me?

I'd watched her walk out of my classroom. She was of medium height and build and that day had on a pleated skirt that stopped just above her knees. As she had got up from the chair in front of me, her skirt had ridden up a little, and her thighs were displayed to me for brief seconds of time: soft, tanned thighs. Thighs I wanted wrapped around my neck.

I pushed my chair backward and got to my feet now my rock hard cock had decided to give it a rest. I gathered my belongings together and decided that swimming tonight was not going to do anything. I needed to get back to my apartment as quickly as possible so that I could watch a porno and jerk myself off.

I caught the subway home to Brooklyn and went into my studio apartment. I loved my modern little home. I had decided after Elvington that I wanted to stand on my own two feet and not use my parents' money to buy my way through life. My mom supported me wholeheartedly. My dad thought I needed committing to an institution. I didn't protest too much though when Mom arranged for the staff to pick up and do my laundry every week. I needed to look smart for work and experience had shown me that I was incapable of doing that all on my own. I'd not realized how dependent I'd been before. I'd gone from living with my parents to living with Eliza, and she had taken over the accounts and run our home in Queens. I wondered if her parents had found her a new rich bachelor to hook up with by now. It was what our families did, tried to marry money with money. When I realized I was free, I went all the way. I stopped accessing the money that my parents refused to take back and set up a separate bank account where I was self-sufficient, settling in my little apartment in Brooklyn. I had figured if I returned to teaching for the last semester, I would get the joy of seeing the students graduate and I would hopefully find my place and my confidence again in teaching, away from the previous drama. A fresh start.

I threw my laptop case down in the hallway and headed straight through to the shower. Fuck the porno; I was hard as a rock again. I would just think of Jennifer Lawrence. It wouldn't be the first time. I stripped off my clothes and left them on the bedroom floor, a perk of living alone. I could do what the hell I wanted. After my shower, I just had to pop those clothes in a laundry bag, and like magic, they would be taken away and then brought back the following day and hung in the closet.

I padded into the bathroom and switched on the shower faucet, running the water until it was just the right side of hot and then I stepped in. I grabbed my washcloth, and hair and shower gel and began to lather myself up. I always felt like I had grime on my skin after a day out in the city. I felt the muscles in the back of my neck and shoulders begin to relax as the heat soaked in. However, the large muscle between my legs still shouted for attention. I soaped up my hands and grabbed my dick, lathering him up. He got harder, which I hadn't thought was possible. If I slipped in the shower, I was going to punch through a wall with this thing. I closed my eyes and let my hand move up and down it. I imagined Jennifer Lawrence in front of me, ready to take me into her willing mouth. Then her face was replaced, and no matter how much I tried to force my imagination to change the picture it was showing me, it stubbornly stayed there like a pen stain on a work shirt. Brown hair in long ringlets came to mind. A pouting mouth encased around my erect dick, warm lips sucking me to the back of her throat. My fist continued to stroke my cock up and down, while I leaned back against the shower wall. In my imagination, large doe eyes looked up at me wanting to know if it was to my satisfaction.

Harder. You can go harder.

I tightened my grip.

Like this? She sucked me with even more force.

Yes, oh yes, just like that.

And then my imagination moved to her lying on my bed, legs wide apart showing me those plump pink folds and her juices flowing as she begged me to fuck her. I nestled myself between those firm thighs, and I plunged into her core. Her heat accepted me, and I stared into those eyes.

Tell me you want me. Say it.

I want you.
I want you...?
I want you, Sir.

My balls pulled back, my cock tightened, and then I felt the rush as cum shot out of me in huge spurts across the shower stall. I collapsed back against the wall again, feeling like I'd run a marathon. My god, I'd never come like that before in my life. Immediately, I felt shame wash over me. I had imagined having sex with a student. After all that had happened at Elvington, I was one day into the new semester, and I had jerked off to thoughts of an English student who I had to spend one-on-one time with on Thursday. I grabbed the shower head and cleaned down the stall, switched the faucet off and left the shower, wrapping myself in a towel. I knew I needed to back out of the arrangement.

To tell Miss. Candy Appleton that I was unable to tutor her.

But I knew as I had the thought there was no way I was strong enough to do that.

That even if I couldn't have her, I didn't want anyone else to tutor her.

That I would be watching closely to see if any other male students were interested in her.

That I'd be looking to see when she was eighteen.

I was in deep shit.

3

CANDY

I had never been so excited to get to school. I straightened my hair with my flat-iron, so it was even longer and applied some product so it gleamed. I didn't want to appear like I was trying to impress too hard though so I dressed in some midnight blue wide-legged pants and a tie-necked white blouse. I finished the look with a pair of velvet mules. As I did daily, I added my vintage Rolex with its peach dial and cream strap.

As usual, Larissa picked me up to take me to school, or rather Jeff did at Larissa's command. I had the whole day to get through before I saw Mr. Newell again.

I sighed out loud, and Larissa turned to me.

"What's with you today, Candy? Did you not sleep well last night? You seem out of it."

I realized I needed to focus on my friends and my

school day so I changed to a subject I knew Larissa would adore—my party.

"My mom is giving me grief about the party. She wants it done her way, all 'grown up,' and she wants adults there. She just wants to show off their wealth again, not me. I've told her what I'd like, but she's not listening."

"Can you not have two parties? One for family and one for friends?"

"Oh, who knows? I'm sick of it all now. I might run away and celebrate my birthday in a McDonalds all by myself."

"No, you won't. If you run away, we'll come with you. Won't we Jeff?"

"Course." Jeff kept his eyes on the road, and I know that if we asked him what we'd been talking about, he'd have no idea. I bet his mind was on driving and some sports game.

"Do you want to grab a burger after school? Get some practice in?" Larissa added.

"I can't. I have to tutor after school," I replied.

"Ah." Larissa's face lit up in amusement. "Now I know why you're so spaced out today. Dreaming about Mr. Newell locking the classroom door and pounding you over the desk."

"Don't be stupid." I flushed.

"What?" Jeff's face turned away from his driving. "She's getting it on with Newell?"

"No, dufus." Larissa shook her head. "She just wants to. Don't you, Candy? So does half the class. He's hot. I'd do him if I didn't have you, honey."

"Yeah, well you do have me so keep your eyes on your books."

"Aw, there's nothing to be jealous of, babe, you're all I want." Larissa pouted at him and then she leaned over and stroked her hand across his dick.

I wanted to puke at the PDA, but instead, I focused on Jeff's jealousy which amused me. Larissa didn't always get the upper hand in that relationship.

The day dragged on. I tried my hardest to focus as I figured that way the hours might speed up, but they never did. I barely ate anything at lunch, I was so nervous about my extra lesson. I drank soda with lots of sugar to keep me awake, plus my mouth was permanently dry. The final bell rang, and I made my way to the bathroom so I could check my appearance.

I reapplied my lip gloss and ran a brush through my hair. I sprayed a mouth freshener inside my mouth so I wouldn't have dog breath and then I stood and appraised myself in the mirror. Good, I looked fresh but not like I'd made a huge effort. Taking a deep breath, I made my way down to Mr. Newell's classroom and knocked on the door.

"Come in," his husky voice directed.

As soon as I pushed open the door, I realised I'd underestimated what my reaction to him would be. My mind had not been able to fully capture the perfection that was Mr. Newell. Now here he was in front of me, looking up from his desk. That perfect hair, along with those blue eyes that had a kindly look about them, but also felt like they could pierce through me like an X-ray. His jacket was on the back of his chair, and the sleeves of his pale-gray shirt were rolled up to the elbow, revealing defined lower arms. I watched as his gaze returned to the books before him and the muscles and tendons beneath that golden skin moved and rippled as he moved the books around.

It seemed like I'd stood there forever staring, but it had been mere seconds. I felt locked in a freeze-frame, happy to stay frozen for the rest of my life.

"Miss. Appleton, take a seat please." He gestured to the desk in front of him. I walked over and sat there, dropping my tote to the floor to my right and then I shrugged out of my jacket, his eyes followed my every move as if he wanted to critique my performance already.

"Can you call me Candy, please, like in class?

Miss. Appleton is what the staff at home call me. I hate it."

"Well, I can assure you that here I'm not your 'staff.' I'm your teacher." Super. I'd only been here about three minutes, and already the teacher was pissed at me.

"I know you're not and I'm very grateful for you agreeing to spend your extra time tutoring me. I hate that we have staff and I hate that they won't call me Candy. I have to say it's mainly my mom's doing." I realized I was talking too much. Mr. Newell didn't give a crap about my home life.

"Sorry. Can we start again? Please could you call me Candy? I'd prefer it."

"Okay." His lip twitched slightly, and I hoped we could move on now. "Well, for the duration of our tutoring, you can call me... Mr. Newell."

I rolled my eyes. "Okay," I replied, finding some confidence from somewhere. "I think I'll be able to manage that somehow."

Within ten minutes we'd settled into a comfortable flow. Mr. Newell was as passionate about teaching the subject of English as I was learning about it and once he saw I was there to focus on getting as much extra understanding of film and literature as I could, his enthusiasm increased.

The lesson finished in what seemed to be record

time. I could have screamed when he said we needed to wrap things up. I'd had the most amazing hour in a long time, spent with a great teacher, learning my favorite subject, and for almost a moment there, but not quite completely, I'd forgotten about my crush.

"I'm happy you're getting tutored, Candy. You have a gift, and any school would be fortunate to have you as an English teacher. That's if you don't make a fortune on your novel."

"I'd have to write it first."

"Why haven't you? Why just notes in a book?" He folded his arms across his chest, and his biceps bulked up. I couldn't help myself; I licked my lips. My mouth was dry again, and I'd not brought a drink in with me.

"I don't know really. I guess it's about committing to that first sentence. I'm scared of where the book will take me, and well, what if it becomes a romance book? I like reading romance, but I think I'd be embarrassed if I wrote one and wouldn't want anyone to read it."

"You're worrying too much." Mr. Newell began to rise from his seat. "Why not start it and see where it goes? Lock it in a drawer, so you know that no one but yourself will have access to it. Write what comes from the heart."

Following his cue, I rose to leave but as I did my head swam, and I felt dizzy. Grasping onto the table, I stood still for a moment while the room stopped spinning.

Mr. Newell was at the side of me in a flash. "Candy. Are you okay?"

He had reached his hand out, and it rested on my shoulder. My skin shivered, and I trembled under his touch. I moved back and waved a hand in front of my face embarrassed. "Yeah, fine. I didn't eat so much today. Didn't have much of an appetite. I'll just grab a candy bar from one of the vending machines in the cafeteria on the way out."

"Hold on. I have an apple. Much better for you," he said. "Sit back down while I get it."

I once again took the seat while he went into his case for the apple. I watched as he rubbed the skin of it down his shirt. Was this supposed to make me less dizzy? I was about to pass out from sheer lust.

He passed me the apple, and I took a bite. Then he laughed.

"What?" I asked, wondering what moronic thing I'd done now.

"I'm just laughing at giving an apple to Miss. Appleton."

"Yeah, yeah, yeah." I sighed. "I've heard it my whole life. Candy apple. My parents suck. Who gives their child a name like that? At least I'll be able to change it when I get married."

He turned away back to his case and started to pack up his belongings.

"Oh my god. I'm sorry, Mr. Newell. I never thought. You probably have a family to get back to, and I'm holding you up." I attempted to get up from my seat again.

He raised a hand at me. "No one to rush back for, so take your time and eat. I'll go get you a drink and then I'll take you home."

"No. No way. That's above and beyond and not necessary. I'll call one of our drivers."

He laughed. "Of course, you would have a driver."

"I sound very spoiled, don't I?"

"It's nothing I'm not used to. Anyway, you won't call a driver because I'm not having a fainting student on my hands. I'll drive you home."

I nodded. "Well I live on East 67th Street, so it's not far."

"I'll go and get you that drink," he repeated before walking out of the room. I watched his retreat and admired his ass which was like a juicy peach encased in cotton. Oh to be his pants!

He returned with a bottle of flavored water, and I drank it down eagerly.

"Thank you."

"Are you feeling okay to leave now?"

I nodded. I was so embarrassed I couldn't get out of there quickly enough.

We walked out of the classroom, and I followed him out to the teacher's parking lot. He unlocked the door of a Chevrolet Impala and opened it for me. I climbed inside. It had a black leather interior and a comfy seat.

"Nice car," I told him.

"Thanks. Have to treat yourself sometimes, right?"

"Sure."

He started the engine, and I sat back in my seat, not knowing what to say now that we were outside of the classroom. For a minute I allowed myself the fantasy that we were a couple and he was taking me home from a date. It was times like this that I could have cursed my parents for living close by the school as we pulled up outside our townhouse in what seemed to have been the blink of an eye.

"Are you okay to get out, or do you want me to help you to the door and tell your mom that you were unwell?"

"Oh my god, no." The words burst out of me before I could consider them. I sat back in the seat looking flushed. "I'm sorry, Mr. Newell, that sounded ungrateful. It's just my mom would lecture me about not eating, when half the time she gets the staff to serve steamed vegetables and fish for dinner because 'we must fit into our clothes well.'" I turned to him. "I'm almost eighteen, Mr. Newell, and my mom needs to start realizing that soon. I hope for a life outside of her world. If you came to the door, she'd treat me like a child, and I'm not."

He nodded, pausing for a moment. "My name is Parker," he told me. "And I'm okay if you call me that in tutoring, but not anywhere else. Sound good?"

I stared at him, my mouth agape. "P-Parker."

He undid the locks.

"Well, I hope you feel better soon, Candy. I'll see you in English on Monday and then for your next tutorial after school Monday. But." He looked at me sternly. "I'll be asking if you ate and if you didn't, I'll send you straight home."

I shook my head in agreement. Though he was right to lecture me, by giving me his first name one minute and scolding me the next he had managed to make me feel like a child again. It was a blunt reminder that he was my teacher and I was a student.

"Night, Mr. Newell," I said, letting him know firmly that I was keeping things professional. Then I left the car and went across the sidewalk and up the steps of our townhouse without looking back.

I ate the dinner prepared for me. Sofia, one of the staff, informed me that my parents were out for dinner for the evening. I excused her to her room, saying I was fine for the night. When I'd eaten, I sat with my head in my hands and thought about my day. I knew I was being a fool over Mr. Newell, but there was something about him which felt beyond a student crush. When his hand had touched my shoulder, I'd felt a shiver throughout my body. I was sure we had a connection. He'd given me no indication of any attraction to me on his part though. I slammed my fist down on the table. It was like my crush three years ago on Justin Bieber. It must be my hormones or something. My mind felt frantic like I needed to calm myself down, to think sensibly. In frustration I ran up to my bedroom, my place of comfort and I threw myself down on my bed and picked up my novel.

Which turned out to be a big mistake.

The main female character of the book had almost been killed in a freak accident. She was unhurt apart from a scrape to her forehead, and after being checked out at the hospital, she'd returned home, where the main male character of the book had vowed to look after her, feeling responsible. The book had been a slow burn, and now it was lit dynamite exploding across the pages. As I read on, I did what I always did when reading: imagined myself as the heroine. But this time the hero had a face too—Parker Newell's.

The characters kissed, and as they did, I pictured Parker and me in the car, the same passion combusting between us like that in the book.

He grabbed my chin in his hands and tilted his face up to look at mine. "My god, you are so beautiful."

My chin trembled under his touch.

"Are you cold? Why are you shivering?"

"I'm shivering because I want you so much."

Somehow the seats magically lowered and there were no uncomfortable parts of the car in the way. We were just wrapped in each other's arms, mouths open and tongues exploring. Our breaths were audible and caused the car windows to steam up. His fingers swiftly unbuttoned my blouse, and he slipped a hand inside my bra, cupping my breast. My nipple pebbled under his touch.

"Is this okay? Tell me this is okay?"

"This is more than okay."

I grabbed his other hand and slipped it under the edge of my skirt. He didn't need any further encouragement. His hand trailed up my thigh, higher and higher, while his mouth continued to devour mine and his fingers pinched my nipple, making me cry out in desperation.

"Please. I need to feel you there."

His fingers slid under the edge of my silky, lace panties and I gasped as he trailed a fingertip through my slick, warm heat.

"So wet. You want me."

"I do. I want you so, so much."

His fingers delved and teased, tickling and tapping my sensitive bud one minute and then entering me the next. I groaned as I felt his digits inside me twisting, seeking out my orgasm. He plunged his fingers in and out of me, while his thumb flicked across my nub.

"Come for me, Candy. Come for me."

"I want you. I need to feel you inside me. Let me do this."

I pulled down his pants and released his shaft. It was huge. In my daydream, there was no virginity, no pain. I took charge. We moved until I was sitting astride him and then I lowered myself onto his cock, filling myself up.

"Oh, Candy. Oh, Christ. You fit me like a glove. I'm not going to last long."

I held onto his shoulders and stared into his eyes as I rode him. Up and down, round and round, until I felt us heading towards our glorious climaxes.

"Fuck, Candy, I'm gonna blow." Parker held on tightly to my hips as he thrust upwards hard and then I lost it, spasming around his glorious cock.

And then I realized where I was. In my bedroom at

home, the book long since thrown to the side on my bedcovers. My panties were down, my fingers inside myself as I recovered from the strongest climax I'd ever given myself. One of my breasts was outside of my bra. I quickly pulled my hand away and pulled my bra cup back up. My face heated. Oh my god, it had all seemed so real. How was I going to face him now, after imagining that had happened between us?

I headed for my shower, to wash away the guilt and shame that had overcome me at my wanton behavior. There was only one thing I could do, and that was to get a date my own age. It was time to see if Julian Murphy did like me and wanted to take me to prom because something needed to come along to redirect my mind and fast. I'd throw myself into dating the jock and concentrating on my birthday party and prom. Maybe I needed to stop the extra tutoring I considered, as I soaped myself up. But I dismissed the thought. I just couldn't bring myself to do it. He couldn't be mine, but I'd value the time I got to spend with him learning more about my favorite subject every week. I *was* talking about the subject of English, *wasn't I?*

4

CANDY

The next morning I headed down for breakfast. My parents were not rushing around for once, though my father's head was behind a business newspaper and lowered just long enough for him to tell me 'good morning.'

My mom patted the seat next to her as if I ever sat anywhere else.

"Now, Candace. I've been doing some planning for your eighteenth. I've booked the top floor of The Norton Hotel. Or rather, the planner I have secured for the event has. She'll be coming to see us this evening, so if you can be in around seven tonight we'll talk menus and themes, though I think themes are rather vulgar and we should just keep everything classy. I certainly want no mention of Belle or getting books as presents. Goodness, Candace. You'll be gifted jewelry not scraps of paper."

"Mother," I shouted. "That's not what I want."

My father dropped his newspaper down again. "Now be a good girl, Candy. Your mom knows exactly how to throw a party, and with her eye for design it will be beautiful."

"Oh, I have no doubt about that," I told him, picking up a glass of orange juice in one hand and a croissant on a plate in the other. "It would just be nice to have my voice heard once in a while."

"Oh, these teenagers, they think they know it all." My mom smiled at my father before turning to me. "One day you'll thank me for not allowing you to embarrass yourself. The photos of the event will be around for the rest of your life you know?"

I felt my forehead crease in frustration. "Mom, I won't be attending this evening. I'm going to the movies after school. You arrange everything with the planner and just let me know where to show up. If you're interested in knowing who I'd like to invite, then please ask, though I'm sure you've already drawn up a list. Then if you could arrange for me to be measured and get me whichever dresses you think would be suitable, I'll just show up like the good little puppet I am."

"Oh, darling, you are overreacting."

"Am I? I'm going back to my room. You're only

interested in what everyone else will think, not about me."

"Candace. You will not speak to your mother like that. We always want what is best for you. Apologize at once."

Though I wanted to smash every item at the table, I knew no good would come of it. I just needed to count down the days until I could escape and attend college.

"I'm sorry, Mother. I know you only have my best interests at heart."

Then I left the room with my glass of orange juice and my croissant, only eating because I didn't want to pass out at school. I was tired of being treated like a damn child. Somehow, and I didn't know how I'd do it yet, I needed people to see me as the adult I was close to becoming.

I went up to my room and ate my breakfast before getting ready, and then I waited for Larissa to text. She was waiting at the curb with Jeff.

"Larissa, I can't take this much longer. They're planning every part of my life. My party, what I'll do when I leave school. I bet my mom even has a list of suitable future husbands."

"Sorry, babe. It sucks, I know. You're just gonna

have to find your own man; preferably a rich one so it closes your mom's mission down and means you can escape."

I turned to Jeff. "Do you think you could let Julian know I might be interested?"

"Sure." Jeff carried on driving.

"Seriously?" Larissa squealed. "You're gonna give him a shot? We can double date!"

I wish my enthusiasm was as high as my best friend's.

"Why not?" I told her, figuring I'd rather double date than have to go anywhere with him on my own. Maybe he'd be an okay guy once I got to know him and I was being judgmental, but all I'd seen was him acting like the girls on his arm were fortunate to be there. I made a silent note in my head that I wasn't going to fall in line. He could chase me. I was going to be different.

"Lar, can we go shopping after school? I told my mom I was going to the movies with you, but I need some new clothes for getting Julian's attention. Maybe a haircut too."

"Candy, oh my god, yes! Let's shop. I love this."

I smiled at her.

"Oh, babe. It's great to see a smile on your face. You'll get the better of your mom one day."

I told her about the plans for my party.

"Well, you know that even though you think it's

boring, everyone will want to be there to celebrate the eighteenth birthday of Candace Appleton, daughter of the great Irena and Art. What you need to make sure is that you outshine your mother completely. So, let's shop for your party too. Don't let her get you a dress. We'll get you one that shows you are all grown up and beautiful."

My heart beat faster with excitement. "You are so right. I'll do what my parents want, what they expect, but I'm going to do it in style."

"Atta girl." Larissa high-fived me.

In the cafeteria at lunch, Julian joined our table. There was me, Larissa, Jeff, and a few others who we regularly hung with, but it was the first time in a while Julian had sat with us. Usually, he sat with the rest of the baseball team, with his most recent ex-girlfriend Brandy hanging around.

He sat diagonally from me. I looked up at him once he'd taken his seat and smiled.

"Hi," he said, and then he engaged another girl at our table in conversation. It was 'Play Hard to Get 101' and was fine with me. I found it quite pathetic, but from tomorrow I was determined that Julian Murphy would be begging me to date him.

After school, I met with Larissa. Jeff, bless him, agreed to drop us off at the mall and pick us up when we were finished, which Larissa assured him wouldn't be any time soon with all the shopping we would be doing and the fact my hair may take a while.

"So, what look are you going for?" she asked me. "What's the vision for the new you?"

"Well." I tilted my hips and pouted. "I need to look grown up, but sexy. Not 'slutty high school tramp' sexy but 'too good for Julian Murphy' sexy. If he wants me, he's gonna have to work for it."

Larissa clapped her hands together. "Oh, Candy. I love this new attitude. Let's shop!" She threaded her arm through mine, and we hit the first store.

With a personal shopper at our disposal, it wasn't long before we found out what worked for me. Tailored pants with a flare at the bottom. Tops that fit against my skin yet looked classy. A sophisticated look, but one that showed my figure off to perfection. I stared at myself in one of the mirrors. My hair was tied up out of the way. I was dressed in a striped white and blue top with flared sleeves. It ended just above my midriff to give a peek of my slender abs without it looking slutty. Fitted white pants with a wider leg led down to a pair of sandals with a small heel. With different hair and make-up, I'd look like a woman, not a schoolgirl. I turned to the personal shopper. "This is exactly what look I was aiming for. You're amazing. Can you bring me anything else that makes me look like this?"

Usually, I barely spent a penny of my allowance, but tonight I was going to max it out.

Ensconced in a chair at a salon I called my mom from my cell.

"Hello, darling. Is everything okay? I'm here with Suki, the planner for your party."

"Yes, Mom. Everything is fine. I wanted to apologize again about this morning. The Norton Hotel will be amazing. Yes also to no theme, but I would like an opulence please and sophistication. Something that shows I'm growing up."

"Oh, honey. That's exactly what I was thinking. Lots of glitz and glamor."

"Perfect. Oh, and Mom. I'm shopping with Larissa, instead of going to the movies. I've spent my allowance, and there are still things I'd like to buy. I'm having a makeover. Is it all right for me to add to your account at Maribel's?"

"Really, darling? Oh, spend away if it's on beautiful new clothes. Your new closet will need filling after all. Shoes, purses, totes; go wild, honey. I have an account at all the main stores so ask them to hold anything you want, and I'll arrange for a driver to come pick everything up for you."

"Thanks, Mom."

"I'll look forward to seeing everything you've

bought. Maybe one night we could go shopping together?"

"Maybe, Mom. I've got to go. I'm having my hair done."

"Speak soon, darling, and leave your party to me. I promise it will be divine."

I ended the call on my cell and turned to Larissa.

"I have an open tab to spend what I like. So, after here, let's get us both expensive dresses for my party. My treat."

Larissa had more than enough money of her own, but she understood why I want to charge her dress to the account also. "Ooh, yes. Can I have shoes and a new purse too?"

"Of course," I agreed. "And some new jewelry. Now sit beside me and have your hair done. Even if it's just a conditioning treatment or a blow out. We're treating ourselves."

The hairdresser ran an almost black, dark-brown color treatment through my hair. It was semi-permanent so that I could see if I liked it before I went the permanent route. Then she cut it to my shoulders, which made the waves of my hair naturally spring up and gave them extra bounce. The color added gloss. As I turned my head from side to side, I imagined the overall look with my new clothes. I was going to blow Parker... I meant, *Julian*, away.

"Makeup next," I informed Larissa.

The mall was closing as we left. My feet ached from all the walking, my body ached from trying on so many outfits, and my mind ached from attempting to avoid thinking about Parker. My crush on my teacher was nothing but an embarrassing schoolgirl infatuation, and I needed to move my focus onto Julian. Once he was eating out of my hand, we might manage a decent date. While he was being an asshole, I wasn't dating him.

What annoyed me most was the fact I knew once my birthday party was announced Julian would be desperate to be my date, and through that gain automatic entry to one of the parties of the year. Well, I wanted him there because he wanted to be with *me*, not because he wanted to be there at the event. So, Operation Candace was now in full force. Yes, my friends and family would still call me Candy, that was all they'd ever known me as, (apart from my mom who refused to ever shorten my name), but inwardly the woman Candace was unfurling, and for once in my life, I was excited by something beyond books and inspirational prose.

On Monday morning, I got ready and made sure I headed down to breakfast early. I was wearing the flare-sleeved striped top and white trousers. My hair hung to my shoulders, dark and glossy, and the product recommended by the salon meant it had soft curls to it which bounced as I walked. Subtle makeup—as shown to me on one of the counters at Maribel's—made my brown eyes look huge and doe-like and my pout was pink.

My mom clapped her hands, and my father almost dropped his newspaper in his breakfast.

"Candace, you look splendid. Twirl, twirl around." My mom circled her finger, and I entertained her by doing so.

"Oh, you look beautiful. Art, doesn't she look stunning?"

My father looked a little lost for words, and my mom crinkled her face up at him.

"Oh, darling. You've noticed your little girl is all grown up." She grasped his hand. "She's almost eighteen, Art, but she's still our little girl. You don't have to worry about her moving on for a while yet."

My father coughed and took a drink of his tea. "You look very elegant, Candy. Only it's a shock to your father seeing you look so grown up."

"Well, as Mom said, I am almost eighteen, and I felt it was time to grow up a little, instead of looking like a studious mouse." I asked the hovering staff for a bowl of fruit, which always pleased my mother. She could be so vacuous sometimes. However, I had my dress for the party, and I needed it to stay fitted to perfection. "Just a black coffee as well, please."

My father returned to his paper, and I chatted to my mom about the plans she'd made for my eighteenth. I told her I would meet with her and the planners from now through to the party date and requested she avoided any extra tutor dates of Mondays and Thursdays.

"Tonight, you could come and look through my new purchases," I told her.

"Yes, darling. Oh, I made some calls. Your closet will be installed by the end of this week." At the moment, my purchases were mainly in a guest room still in their packaging. I closed my eyes and said a mental goodbye to my library, vowing that when I had my own place, it would be the first thing I arranged. "That's fantastic," I told her. "Right, I need to get ready for school." I rose from the table, kissed her and my father on the cheek and went to grab my new tote and wait for Larissa and Jeff.

"Girl, you look sensational," Larissa declared. Even Jeff, who was usually so quiet on the journey to school to allow us to gossip, opened his eyes wide. "Candy, you look hot. Julian is going to come in his pants when he sees you."

"Jeff!" Larissa scolded. Jeff just shrugged and started the engine.

"Bring it on," I whispered to Larissa. "Julian can do what he likes today. I'm not going to notice."

"Oh, I love this." Larissa giggled. "School just got way much more fun."

I was the hot topic of conversation at school. The girls all wanted to know where my clothes were from, who did my hair, and no doubt bitched about me behind my back. The boys stared, and I got some wolf-whistles. I saw Julian's jaw drop just before I turned on my heel and walked in the opposite direction to where he was.

This time when it came to the seating arrangements at lunch, Julian stood at the side of me.

"Is this seat taken, Candy?"

I turned to him and looked at the empty seat next to me. "Looks free to me," I said, then as he took it, I turned my back to him, so I was facing Larissa. My best friend was dying not to laugh.

I felt a tap on my back, and with an eye-roll, I turned back around.

"Yes?" I looked Julian up and down, letting him know I was checking *him* out to see if he was good enough for *me*.

"I was just wondering about prom," he said.

I looked at my watch. "Were you? Shoot. Is that the time? Lar, come on, we need to get to the gym." I gave her a stare that meant go along with whatever I said.

"Gosh, yes." She jumped up, abandoning the rest of her sandwich.

"Catch you later," I told the rest of the table, and we were on our way.

"I'll get you another sandwich later," I apologized. "But I needed to leave Julian hanging."

"Got ya, babe. You should have seen his face. He looked so pissed." She guffawed. "I love it. Now, I guess we aren't going to the gym?"

"You have met me before, haven't you? Go to the gym? Hahaha. No, let's go to the bathroom so I can check my appearance. It's English next," I winked.

"Candace Appleton, are you going to flirt up a storm with Mr. Hotty-pants Newell?"

I winked. "I don't do things like that, Miss. Davenport"

"I don't think I know what you do or don't do anymore. You're becoming a new woman."

"Emphasis on the woman," I told her. "No going back. I no longer accept being treated like a child."

5

PARKER

I'd been restless all day, knowing that after lunch she'd be in my class and that after school we had yet another private tutoring session. I had my best shirt on—how pathetic was that? *Not as pathetic as the fact that you're a teacher lusting after one of your students*, I berated myself.

Then she walked into the room, and my heart almost stopped. A young student had left my room the other day, but a full-blown woman had walked into my classroom right now. Her hair was a couple of shades darker and glossy and a few inches shorter; her makeup made her face look sculptured, just perfect, accentuating those innocent looking eyes and that delicate rosebud pout. I wanted to destroy that innocent face by plowing my cock straight down her throat while those eyes looked up at me begging for more. My dick twitched in my pants, and I had to take a seat at my desk, so that no one noticed the hard-on I was now sporting. Just the way she strolled into the classroom was different today. It was a move of confidence, of self-assuredness. She knew how good she looked and was owning it.

I waited for her to catch my eye. It wouldn't have been the first time one of my female students had changed their appearance and then tried to parade themselves in front of me, desperate for my attention. Had Candy made this change for me? Had she got a crush on me? Yet her face never came up and looked at mine. She was engaged in chatter with Larissa Davenport and other students who were desperate to speak to her. She commanded them all, and I noticed a few of the male students trying to get her attention and passing comment to each other about her. I saw one mouth the word, 'Hot,' and felt my jaw tighten.

"Samuel, did you bring your homework in?" I found myself pissed at him for acknowledging what I had seen too. Yet, he could actually try to do something about it. He could ask her out, date her, *fuck her*.

Dear God, what was I thinking? Here as the responsible adult and wondering about her being nailed by another student. But something had changed in a short space of time for this transformation to occur and I wondered if it related to the conversation we'd had when I'd dropped her off Thursday after her tutoring, about her being frustrated with being treated as a child. She'd made me well aware right now that she was not a child.

Too aware.

"Here, Sir."

"Hmm, what?"

"The homework you asked for?" Samuel said, looking at me strangely.

I took it from him. "Thanks." I dismissed him quickly, still annoyed at him for no valid reason.

While I waited for the last of the class to file in, I wondered what it was about Candy that appealed to me so much? I had other students who were pretty, dressed well, looked older than they were. None of them had ever caused the remotest flicker of either my heart or my dick. But from the moment I'd seen Candy, my heart felt like it was going to burst from my chest and my dick was in danger of blowing out my zipper.

"Class. If you can open your books to page 326 and start there, I'll be back in a moment," I told them.

I went into the—thankfully empty—male staff restroom and went into a stall, locking it firmly behind me. Standing in front of the toilet, I unzipped my fly and took my cock in my hand. It needed a release so much it was painful. Gripping myself firmly, I jerked myself off furiously, already so near to a climax that within a few tugs I spurted into the bowl. It had been so fervent that afterward I had to lean against the stall door for a moment while I caught my breath and my equilibrium.

I had to get it together.

I cleaned myself up, splashed my face with cold water and called down to the cafeteria for a cold drink as if that was all I'd left the classroom for. When I returned, some of my class was doing as I'd asked, but most were chatting. Only one person watched as I walked back to my desk.

Her.

Our eyes met, but she quickly looked away. There'd been no sign of what she was thinking in her gaze. It was utter torment.

The rest of the lesson passed unremarkably and Candy never seemed to look my way again. I wrapped up the class, and as the bell rang, I stared after her, ready to say I'd see her after classes ended. But she left the classroom from the back, chatting to a friend and never once looked my way. I wasn't even sure at that point if she was going to show up for our session.

And although it would perhaps be for the best if she skipped, I didn't want to acknowledge how much it would hurt if she didn't show.

6

CANDY

"He could not stop looking at you," Larissa whispered. "I think Mr. Newell has the hots for you."

"Don't be stupid. He'll just be wondering why I look different."

"His face said he wanted to fuck you."

I folded my arms. "How does a face look like that?" I laughed.

Larissa stuck her eyes out like they were on stalks and licked around her mouth in an over-exaggerated pervert-like way.

"Oh my god, Lar. If he looked at me like that, I'd send for the psychiatrists."

"Well, don't be surprised if he gives you detention for no reason." She clapped a hand over her mouth. "Oooh, you have your extra lesson tonight, don't you? What will you do if he makes a move?"

"Sshh." I attempted to quieten her down. "One, he does not have feelings for me. Two, he's a teacher! Three, he'd lose his job if he did. Four, I'm going to learn more about English."

"You are such a spoilsport. Please flirt with him a bit and see what he does."

"No." I chastised her. "I have my eye set on Julian being my date for prom. That's it for my romantic life. Let's keep it realistic and uncomplicated."

"Boring, you mean?" she said.

"Yes, boring," I told her.

Usually, I told Larissa everything, but I couldn't bring myself to tell her the truth. That the real reason behind my makeover was because I wanted Parker to look at me like I was a woman, not a student. That deep inside I wanted my teacher, no matter how wrong and forbidden it was. That it had been easy to turn my back on Julian because he meant nothing to me and I just saw my behavior toward him as karma for what he'd done to his previous girlfriends.

I left Larissa and went off to my next class. Soon I found myself walking back to Mr. Newell's classroom.

"Come in," his gruff voice once again answered my knock.

He straightened his tie as I walked in. "There's no need to knock, Candy, I'm expecting you. Come on in, take a seat."

I repeated what I'd done on Thursday, but this time I walked over with confidence as if I was his equal, not his student. I placed my tote on a chair at the side of me, rather than dropping it to the floor and I crossed a leg over the other and sat back.

"I never asked you on Monday, forgive my manners, but did you want anything toward the gas?" I asked.

"What? Oh, no. Not at all. How are you anyway? No more fainting episodes?"

"No, I've made sure I've eaten properly," I told him and then lost my cool a little and rambled on, "Now I permanently have something crammed in my mouth."

He swallowed. I watched his Adam's apple rise and fall, and he adjusted his tie again as if it was choking him. I flushed bright red. *Candy, you idiot.* I chastised myself. *So not cool.*

"Right. I thought we'd look at deus ex machina," he said. And the lesson began.

We were awkward around each other.

The friendliness and joint enthusiasm for our subject from just a few days before had disappeared. Parker went into complete professional teacher mode, and I stayed cool and aloof while I answered. My appearance was supposed to have made him see me as a woman, but it appeared the opposite had occurred. He'd become more professional than ever.

At the last tutor session he'd almost seemed like an older friend, a mentor, but today there was none of that.

When it came to the end of the lesson, I gathered my things away quietly.

"Thank you," I said to him. "I'll see you on Thursday? Same time?"

"Yes." He nodded, then he turned back to put his belongings away.

"Are you walking out?" I pointed toward the door.

"No. I have a few things to sort out before I leave. You go on ahead."

I nodded and gathered up my tote and headed toward the door.

I was halfway through it when I heard my name. So softly, if the door had creaked, I'd have missed it.

"Candy."

I turned, my face schooled into a mask that gave nothing away.

"You look really nice. Your hair and your clothes. Very smart. I think your mother will come to realize you're not her little girl anymore soon if she hasn't already."

I ran a hand down my top as if seeing my clothes again through his eyes.

When I looked up, he watched me. His eyelids were hooded, his pupils dark. He was interested. Oh my fucking god. He was interested, whether he was willing to do something about it or not.

"Thanks, Sir," I said, cruelly reminding him he was my teacher as a form of punishment for the fact he'd kept me beyond arms-length for the whole of the lesson. I knew it was forbidden, the relationship between teacher and student, but right now I resented that if he felt about me the way I felt for him, he didn't have the classroom door slammed and me pinned up against it.

His eyes widened as he realized I knew how he felt. That he'd given me a clue.

"Candy, I—"

I knew I was about to get some rejection speech, so I quickly looked at my watch. "Shoot, is that the time? I've gotta run," I said, in almost identical words to my conversation with Julian at lunch.

The door closed behind me, and although I felt like running, I walked to the car lot where our driver was waiting for me.

I slept terribly that night, tossing and turning and dreaming of a fight at my party between Parker and Julian. I was determined to keep up my new appearance, so I made sure my concealer did its job and masked the dark rings under my eyes. I was at my locker in the afternoon when Julian came over.

"Hey, Candy."

This time I had to talk to him. He was right there at the side of me, and I didn't have the energy to rush off. I stuffed my belongings back in my locker while I turned to him.

"Julian, hey."

I looked him over. He was good looking, there was no doubt about it, and he wore shorts that highlighted the definition in his calves. Baseball did good things to his body. His skin glowed with its healthy golden tan, and his blond hair shone with highlights that his friends got from chemicals at salons, and he got from fresh air and the sunshine.

He smiled at me, revealing his perfect white teeth. He'd definitely not been born with those, but then neither had most of our school.

"I wondered if you'd like to catch a movie sometime?" he asked.

I was about to turn him down when Parker appeared at the other end of the hall. He froze in place watching me talk to Julian.

"Sure," I told Julian. "That sounds fun. Maybe we could double date with Larissa and Jeff and go to the Surf Shack afterward?"

"Sounds great," Julian replied. "Tomorrow night? If that's okay with the others?"

By this time Parker had walked down the hall toward us, and he strolled on by, right past where we were standing.

"I'm sure tomorrow night will be fine. It's a date," I told him, and I watched Parker flinch at my words. Then he picked up his pace and walked off down the hall.

Julian grinned at me as he walked away. "I'll wait to hear from you."

"Okay."

I stood with my head against the locker as my mind whirled with what just happened. Did Parker come down the hall deliberately to hear what we were talking about? I headed off to my lesson. I was so confused about everything.

―――

On Wednesday, Larissa and Jeff had said they were fine with our double date, and we were all set for after school when Julian came rushing over to us in the cafeteria.

"Candy. I'm so sorry. I can't do tonight." He looked pissed and frustrated. "I got after school detention."

"Seriously?" I asked him. Julian had never in all the time I'd known him caused any trouble in class.

"Yeah, that new teacher, Newell. He's a dick."

I felt like my heart dropped into my stomach at his name.

"I only reached for a spare pen from Tate's desk, and he accused me of cheating on the test we were doing. It was only a mock. The guy's a total dick. I'm so sorry, Candy. Can we reschedule for tomorrow?"

I shook my head. "I have extra class tomorrow from school. Friday?"

"Sure." He leaned over and kissed my cheek. "Sorry about that. Oh, and I got the invite to your party. I didn't realize you were eighteen next week. Not a lot of notice for one of the parties of the year."

"That's my mother for you. Does everything last minute to create drama and chaos."

"Well, I'll be there. Maybe even as your date?"

I nodded. "We'll see how Friday goes, but yes, if you like, you can be my date for the following Friday too."

He smiled, and I watched as he dashed off to class. Maybe I'd misjudged Julian. He seemed like a nice guy. I needed to focus on him and not Parker Newell. But why else would Parker have kept Julian after school if not to ruin my date?

7

CANDY

I woke determined. I was attending my after school tutor session, and I didn't yet know how, but I was going to discover if Parker Newell, definitely, for a fact, was interested in me. I couldn't in good conscience date Julian—as much as he seemed a great guy—if I had even the remotest chance to get up close and personal with my teacher.

I dressed in a black eyelet peplum top and a wrap mini-skirt that hit just above my knees.

Julian couldn't stop telling me how fantastic I looked. The rest of the school had heard we were dating and when he sat next to me in the cafeteria at lunch, I noticed a lot of dagger eyes from other girls, especially Brandy. We chatted nonsense, like what we were going to eat at the Surf Shack and mock-argued about which movie we would all see. Larissa and Jeff joined in the chat, and it was nice finding myself part of the crowd. My upcoming birthday party was also a hot topic of conversation, with other students telling me their parents had cancelled vacations in order to attend. I found it all incredulous, but it showed how much influence my parents had on the Upper East Side. I wondered if anyone would notice if the 'Belle of the Ball' failed to make an appearance? Then I remembered the outfit I'd purchased, and I smiled to myself. My mother had no idea. She'd had dresses sent to the house and had chosen one for me. I wouldn't be wearing it. Her choice was demure and for a daughter of a prominent power couple of New York. Mine was the dress of a woman who now knew the power of playing to your strengths.

After school, I went to Parker's classroom and pushed open the door without knocking.

"Hey, Parker," I said, waving a general hand in his direction. Then I took my seat and once again crossed one leg over the other, this time revealing the top of my thigh.

"I thought we'd look at improvisation today," he said to me, like I was dressed in a nun's habit.

"Whatever you think. You're the teacher," I replied, and I bit my lip.

His eyes wavered, watching me as I licked across

my bottom lip before he put his face back down to his papers.

"So, can you recall any instances where on Broadway improvisation has been used to good effect?"

"Gimme a sec. It's hot in here today, isn't it?" I answered, and then I pulled down my top a little, revealing a hint of the tops of my creamy white breasts and I blew down my top. I recalled a seduction scene in a book I'd read a couple of weeks previously, and the devil in me began to act it out.

"Improvisation?" he reminded me, though a smirk tugged at the corner of his top lip.

I gave him a complete and concise answer to his question. I think we both knew that my asking for his help had been a lack of confidence in my abilities. I was acing the subject.

"Perfect, Candy," he told me. "Just... perfect." I wasn't sure if we were talking about my answer anymore.

He gave me a small written assignment and set a time of fifteen minutes to do it. I made sure I tucked my hair behind my ear and that I kept sucking on the end of the pen, or biting it as if in deep thought. Parker stayed mainly hidden behind the screen of his laptop, though when he did look up, I felt his gaze burn through me.

At the end of the fifteen minutes, he walked over

and stood at the side of the desk, brushing past me. I felt his thigh against my naked arm: the brush of the material of his pants and the heat from his body. "Are you finished?" he asked.

I leaned over slightly to pick up my paper knowing it would give him, should he be looking, a direct view of my breasts encased in my lacy white bra.

"I'm not sure, Parker." I handed it over to him. "You tell me if I'm finished."

The paper came out of my hand and floated across the floor, as the top of my arm was grasped and I was dragged toward the back of the classroom out of view of the windows.

The next thing I knew I was pressed up against the wall as Parker Newell's hand trailed down the side of my face.

He stared into my eyes. I should have been nervous, but I wanted this too much.

"What you do to me? I can't bear it," he said.

He held my chin and tilted my head up to his and then his face came forward, and he crushed his lips to mine. It was like fireworks exploded in my body. So many sensations, things I'd never experienced before, converged on me. I felt like my lips had electric shocks from their contact with Parker's. I wrapped my arms around his neck as his tongue forced entry into my mouth. Everything I'd read about in my romance novels, even the ones that had made my body react, did not come close to what was happening right now. I felt my panties dampen as my juices flowed from my core. Parker's hand dipped underneath my top, and his fingers trailed feather-light touches up my flesh, causing goose bumps. As he reached the edge of my bra, I felt him hesitate for a brief moment, so I grabbed his hand with my own and placed it over the cup of my lacy number. He groaned into my mouth while he slid his hand down inside the cup of my bra and cupped the flesh there. My nipple hardened as he stroked it with his fingertips, coaxing it into bud. I was breathing hard against his mouth.

Then he pushed me away and backed off as if I'd burned him.

"I can't do this. We can't do this. My job." He ran a hand through his hair, his face creased in torment. "I'm sorry, Candy. So, so, sorry. If you want to report me, go ahead. What I've done is completely inappropriate."

I moved towards him and grasped his hand.

"I don't want to report you. I feel the same. Please, can't we keep it secret?"

He shook his head vehemently. "You're seventeen, Candy."

"I'm eighteen in eight days." I pleaded with him. "This can't be wrong; it felt too right."

But it was too late, the shutters came down across Parker's face, and he rushed towards his belongings.

"I'm sorry, again, Candy."

"Tell me you don't have feelings for me," I demanded.

He shrugged. "It wouldn't make any difference. I'm your teacher. I can't give you extra tutoring any more, Candy. It's not appropriate. You don't need it anyway. It's more than obvious that you are amazing in English. You'll make one hell of a teacher or a novelist. I trust whichever path you take you'll excel. I'll still see you in English, but please don't make this any more difficult for me than it already is. Date Julian. He's your age. He's what you need."

"You're what I need." Frustration made a tear slip from the corner of my eye.

He shook his head again. "I'm not. Now please leave."

I gathered up my belongings. Parker indicated my top, and I realized my bra was visible. I hastily pulled up my top, and then I ran from the classroom straight to the nearest bathroom where I locked myself in a stall and cried until I was heaving with dry sobs.

After a while, I realized that I needed to get home. I washed my face and reapplied my makeup to disguise my puffy red eyes as best as I could. I pushed the bathroom door open slightly and peered around to make sure he wasn't nearby and then I went home. I faked a headache and asked for dinner to be sent to my room. My parents were going out anyway, so they didn't check up on me. I spent my evening tormenting myself as I replayed what happened in my mind. He'd kissed me. I touched my fingertips to my lips. He'd felt my breast. I climbed into bed, closed my eyes and imagined the whole thing again, but let my imagination take it further as I used my hands. I imagined his touch between my legs, and it brought me to an orgasm. When I came again, shame, regret, and devastation flooded my senses. What if he never touched me again? I didn't think I could bear it. I cried myself to sleep.

I woke and slowly the events of the evening before washed over me. The fact it was the last day of the school week was reassuring. If I could just survive the day, then I had the weekend to think things over. Then I remembered it was the double date. Good, I thought. Maybe I'd have fun with Julian and thoughts of Parker Newell would disappear from my mind. I got out of bed with renewed vigor. I would look fabulous. If Parker saw me, he would think I was unaffected by what he'd done. It was time to move on. My eighteenth birthday was approaching, and it was a time for celebration, not to be miserable.

I fixed my hair in a ponytail which swung as I moved and I wore a cute top decorated with pink love hearts and a pair of cream cut offs.

"Hey, Lar, Jeff," I greeted my friends at the curb. "You still on for the date tonight?"

"Yeah. As long as it's *Guardians of the Galaxy*," Jeff said. "I'm not watching any of that girly stuff."

"Guardians sounds good," I said, as Larissa and I gave each other a look that we knew meant that even if the film were utter garbage it had Chris Pratt in it, so we'd enjoy it anyway.

"So, movie, then Surf Shack?" Jeff checked.

"Yeah, baby. I love a good old surf n turf." Larissa rubbed her stomach. "I'll be glad when your party is out of the way, honey, so I can eat properly again."

"You girls. Dieting to fit in dresses. Crazy," Jeff said.

"You say that but would you still want me if I was huge?" Larissa asked.

"Yeah, I'd dive into your doughy flesh and never come up for air," he replied.

We laughed. Then I sat back in the car and watched the two of them. They were so in love. I bit my lip hard to stop a tear from forming.

The movie was fantastic and eased me into our

date. I'd seen nothing of Parker all day which had both disappointed me and made me feel relieved. We'd sat in the cinema: Jeff, Larissa, me, and Julian. Julian had bought both of us a drink and some popcorn to share and other than the odd bit of general conversation we'd just watched the movie. On the way out and as we walked to the Surf Shack, he'd taken hold of my hand. I'd let him. It felt nice. He sat alongside me in our booth, opposite the others, and again in between food arriving he kept holding my hand.

"This time next week we'll all be at your party, Candy. I don't think we'll be as comfortable then," Larissa said.

"No." I sighed. "We'll be in dresses we can barely breathe in, while our every movement is watched by our parents."

"Ah shoot, do I have to wear a suit?" Jeff joked, when I knew he had it all ready to go.

"We've got to accompany these fine women and make sure our clothes complement their outfits. What color is your dress, by the way, so I can get a tie to match?" Julian asked.

"Silver," I told him. "So, silver or grey will do." I turned to him. "You do know that my parents, especially my mother, will have me mingle with every guest, so I'll be lucky if I get to spend much time with my actual friends."

Larissa looked at me, her face a world of understanding. It was how the Upper East Side worked. My mother may as well put me on the top of a huge cake. I was just a display.

"We'll make time," she reassured me.

"Yes, we'll steal you away," Julian said. "I'll want some alone time with the birthday girl so I can give you your present."

"Oooh," Larissa exclaimed.

I went bright red, but it didn't bother Julian at all.

"Miss. Davenport, take your mind out of the gutter. I haven't even kissed the lovely Miss. Appleton yet."

He picked up my hand and kissed the back of it. "Though there's a start."

I felt all shivery as his mouth left the slightest moistness on the back of my hand. When we left, would we all head home together or would Larissa and Jeff leave us? Would Julian want to kiss me?

I became so nervous, I barely ate my main course, bringing the headache out as an excuse for the second day in a row.

Sure enough, Larissa and Jeff said their goodbyes and Julian agreed to take me home. He drove me back in his Lexus and pulled up further down the street.

"I'll walk you to your door in a moment, but first I want to do this," he told me. Then he leaned over and kissed me. His lips landed clumsily on mine at first, but then we tilted our heads together and found a steady rhythm. His mouth was soft and warm, and when he tried to put his tongue in my mouth, I let him. He tasted of hickory sauce. He didn't try anything else. It was nice. That was all I had to say about it. Nice. There was no passion awoken in me like when Parker kissed me. Maybe it was the fact my kiss with Parker was forbidden and that made it hotter?

We broke the kiss and then Julian walked me to the house.

"So, can I take you out again?" he asked.

"I have so much going on this week getting ready for the party, so can our next date be the party itself? I'll have more time when that's out of the way," I told him.

He looked disappointed for a moment and then he rallied. "Sure. Plus, I'll see you at school too. When your party is out of the way, maybe we can go out, just the two of us?"

"That sounds nice," I told him. There I was again with that word.

He kissed me on the cheek and walked back down the sidewalk to his car. I waved to him and was about to go into my house when I saw him, right across the street.

Parker.

I stared at him.

He stared at me.

I was about to turn and walk up the steps to my door when I saw him put up a hand. He beckoned to a restaurant down the street. All of a sudden, my appetite returned. But was it for food, or for Parker?

As I stood there, he crossed the street.

"Come to dinner with me."

I peered around. "What if someone sees us?"

His posture was stiff, muscles rigid. "I don't care."

"Parker. You could lose your job. You were right. What we did last night was foolish. You need to leave me alone. I have a boyfriend now."

"That child?" His jaw was set, and he spat out the words.

"He's a few months older than I am, so thanks for clarifying what you think about my age."

"You need a man, not a boy."

Tension knotted my neck and shoulders. "I need to not bring shame to my family for kissing my teacher." I spat back. "Now if you'll excuse me, I haven't seen them since early yesterday evening."

He grasped my hand.

"It's killing me," he said.

"What?" I whimpered, suddenly having lost my fire.

"I want you so goddamn badly. I'll wait. You're eighteen in a week. It's all over school about your celebration. One week. Please don't do anything with Julian Murphy. I couldn't bear it."

"It's not allowed, Parker," I said, withdrawing my hand. My head dropped to the floor as his gaze was too intense.

He lifted my chin up, forcing me to look at him. "I'll see you Monday. In class and afterward," he said, his voice choked with emotion.

"Class, yes. Afterward, no. You were right. I don't need any more tutoring."

"Candy." He wrung his hands.

"Leave me alone, Mr. Newell," I said. "School's out for the weekend."

I ran up the steps and into my house.

On Monday, I skipped school so I didn't have to go to his English class. The rest of the week was a blur of last minute preparation for the party and all my spare time at school was filled between Larissa and Julian. Before I knew it, it was Friday once again.

I was now eighteen years old.

8

CANDY

I jumped out of bed and peeled back the drapes. I noticed there was a large pink bow across the adjoining door between my room and what was now to be my closet. I pulled off the bow and pushed open the door and stood there looking at the sheer luxury of the interior of my new closet. Everything was split into sections for different pieces of clothing. There were large mirrors, a grand chandelier, and a rack that held my shoes. All my new purchases were hanging there, along with other brand-new items. There was one section of the closet packed with totes and purses, all brand new. I stared at them: Chanel, Prada, Balenciaga.

My feet walked across the plush carpet as I stared at the rows. There was no doubt about it; my mother had outdone herself and, had my image been everything to me, I would have felt like I'd died and gone to heaven. However, though it was amazing, and the clothes and accessories seemed exactly my style, it was just dressing up. It was focused on the outside of me, and I thrived on focusing on the inside. "Candy, don't be so ungrateful," I said to myself. As I reached the end of my new closet, I saw another bow across a closet door. What on earth could be inside this one? I didn't think there was anything I didn't have. I pulled it open.

It wasn't a closet door.

It was a *fake* closet door.

My mouth dropped open.

Through the fake door, was a library. There were bookshelves all around the room. My feet took on a mind of their own, and I ran around the periphery. Although a lot of the shelves were empty, I found first editions of many classics. Also in the room, there was a beautiful antique chinoiserie pedestal desk and an Edward Wormley chaise longue. The whole place was filled with massive vases of flowers and large balloons with '18' on them. My mother's interior design talent had brought my dreams to life.

My hand was across my mouth. I was speechless. Tears threatened to pour from my eyes. My mind whirled with emotions. I was overwhelmed, my senses spinning.

I dressed quickly in an Alexander Wang peplum shift dress I'd spotted hung in my new closet, slipped my feet into Sergio Rossi studded suede sandals and ran down the landing and staircase into the dining room where I threw my arms around first my mother and then my father.

"Oh my god, thank you so much," I said to them. I was almost dancing around the room, and I didn't care. My father for once did not have his head hidden behind a newspaper and I saw the table was decorated with the best china.

"Come. Sit for your birthday breakfast." My mother reached for a glass. "Here, don't tell school but it's mimosa for breakfast made with Armand de Brignac gold champagne and fresh oranges from Union Square."

I took the glass, and my mom and dad raised their glasses. "Let's raise a toast." My father said. "To our beautiful eighteen-year-old daughter. We are so very proud of you, sweetheart, and hope you get everything in life you wish for."

"I already had one of them granted this morning." I beamed. "Mom, the closet is beautiful, but my library—there aren't enough words to express how I feel about it."

"Ironic given it's a library." My mom laughed. "It was your father's idea. After I had shown him the closet, he said why didn't we just continue through that part of the house. It worked out splendidly. We did consider carrying on further with a living area, but then I felt we'd never see you, so I vetoed that idea."

"I have everything I need up there: my room, my closet, my library. I will make it downstairs for food and to see my parents."

"Glad to hear it," my father said. "Now, while we wait for our breakfasts, why don't you open your other gifts."

My father passed me a gold envelope. Inside was a store card for the largest bookstore in New York.

"Fill your shelves whenever you like. Any editions you would like them to search for, there's the business card of their acquisitions person inside the envelope."

My eyes went wide. My mother passed me another envelope. The same thing for three of the finest clothes emporiums of the Upper East Side.

"And now this." My mom passed me a blue box with a white bow. Tiffany's. Inside was the most beautiful bangle bracelet in white gold. Etched with a feather design.

My mouth dropped open. It matched my eighteenth birthday dress. The one I'd kept hidden.

"Mom."

"I saw the dress during the renovations. I'm afraid I know all the tricks about hiding purchases. I used to do it with your father before our wealth increased and I no longer had to hide anything."

My eyes sought reassurance from hers that everything was all right.

"The dress is beautiful, and you are going to look sensational. I called Romana and sent her details, and she has changed your hair and makeup plans to complement the change of outfit. She'll be here at four thirty, so you should hurry home from school."

"I will. Thank you for everything. My birthday has already been like a dream."

"Well, we realized that at any time soon, you could have your own career, your own family, and your own home. While you're still here, we want you to have everything you desire. Maybe I'm being soft, but I guess it's our bribery to keep you here a little longer," my father said. "However, everything we have had fitted moves. The whole of the closet, the whole of the library. When and if you marry and move out, you can take them with you."

I was even more dumbstruck. In fact, the whole of the morning felt surreal. I'd thought my parents were largely disinterested in my life and yet here they were celebrating my birthday. My gifts were amazing, and my mom was allowing me to wear the dress I thought she'd make me change out of the minute she saw it.

I got ready for school and ran to the door when I heard a beep.

When I went outside, I'd thought it was strange that my parents followed me to the door.

Parked in front of the house was a Porsche Boxter RS60. Though able to drive, I'd never asked for a car as Jeff took me to school and I had a driver at my disposal the rest of the time. But here it was. Larissa and Jeff jumped out of his jeep parked in front, and she ran over to me hugging me toward her and squealing. "Happy birthday, BFF."

"This is from you?" I shrieked.

"Well, it's from my parents, but on behalf of me. I have lots of other things for you too, but mainly I asked them for this because you need your own wheels, babe." She leaned over me and whispered, "Can't have clandestine affairs with teachers if you have to tell the driver where you're going."

"Larissa!"

She winked.

"Okay, you're driving yourself to school." She threw the keys at me. "I'm ditching Jeff and riding shotgun. Let's go."

I ran around to the driver's seat and threw my tote in the footwell. I stroked my hands down the all red interior. "I can't believe you got me a car!"

Larissa jumped in. "I know, I'm amazing." She giggled, and with a wave at my parents, we were on our way to school.

School passed relatively quietly as other students were bringing their gifts to my party, though we gossiped non-stop about my presents received so far. What amused me was it was the Upper East Side, and a personal library was tame in comparison to some of my classmates own eighteenth birthday gifts: exclusive intimate concerts with top pop stars, some had been bought their own homes and islands. I hoped that although I was around ridiculous wealth, my main gift kept me grounded. Books travelled along every level of society. The gift of reading kept on giving. I vowed to do a fundraiser soon for people who were unable to read.

Julian had sat at my side at lunch and excitedly told me that I would love his gift.

While I was eating my lunch, my cell buzzed. It had been happening all day with messages arriving from family and friends who couldn't make the party but sent me their best wishes. I almost ignored it, but unopened texts and messages made me antsy, so I pulled it from my tote.

Unknown number: Happy birthday, Candy. I hope it brings you everything you

have dreamed of. I want to give you my address. If you ever need me for anything, I'm here: 250 West 50th Street. P x

I threw it back in my tote like it was made of molten lava. I couldn't deal with thoughts of Parker today.

I stood in front of the mirror and could hardly believe my reflection. The dress I had purchased had a skin tone colored lining, making it appear I was naked below the fine lacy silver spun overlay. It had a sweetheart neckline, sleeves that tapered out to a slight flare at the wrist and it fit me like a glove down to my feet where again it flared out slightly. The elasticity of the outfit meant that it moved with me and wasn't difficult to move around in. The silver overlay was a fretwork of feathers; it had reminded me of a pen quill when I had seen it. My hair had been straightened, pulled back behind one ear and waved to emulate a movie star style from the olden days. I had smoky eyes, outlined with black kohl; and fake eyelashes and a red lip completed the look. For jewelry, it had been kept simple with my bangle, and a jeweled clip that held the side of my hair back. The stylist felt the dress was enough of a jewel.

My feet were encased in crystal embellished sandals, and I had a small black purse containing only my car keys and my cell. I wasn't sure why I'd even bothered with a purse, but I didn't feel complete without one.

When my father saw me, he spluttered and told my mother I needed to get changed. She'd had to get a scotch organized for him to calm down his raised blood pressure.

The party progressed without a hitch. Every element organized to perfection. There was a well-known DJ entertaining the dance floor and magicians brought in from Las Vegas worked the seated crowds.

Julian arrived with his parents. An only child, his father was also a politician, though less prominent than my own, and his mother an ex-beauty queen. They walked over to where I stood with my parents.

Julian's eyes almost bulged out of his sockets when he saw me. His mother swept in to kiss both of my cheeks, and his father shook my hand. Then they did the same with my parents.

"Meghan, you look beautiful as ever." My mother exchanged pleasantries.

"Thanks, Irena, but I feel old and relegated to the

shadows next to this exquisite creature." She gestured toward me. "Julian, darling, please give our gift to Candy."

"Oh, yes, here." Julian handed me a glittery silver envelope. I opened it and extracted three tickets to a ballet performance next week.

"For you and your parents. In our box, of course."

"Oh, thank you so much, that's very generous," I said courteously. I had zero interest in ballet, but it was a lovely gesture.

"We'd be honored to join you there," my mother replied.

"Well, with these two dating, we should get to know each other. You never know, we could be organizing an engagement party next."

I looked in horror at Julian. We'd only had one date, but he looked from his parents to my own and smiled.

"I would be very fortunate if that should happen in the future," he said. "Now, if it's okay with you, I'd like to take my girl onto the dance floor."

I danced with Julian, though I was frustrated about what had just occurred. Then I began to calm as I guessed he was under pressure from his parents. I also danced with Larissa and Jeff, and other friends. The night went on, and I noticed Julian appeared a little off. He became a little cocky and seemed too relaxed.

"Are you okay?" I asked him.

"I'm amazing, babe," he replied. "I have the most beautiful woman here on my arm. I am a little overheated though. Shall we go outside for a while?"

"Is there an outside?" I asked him. I'd not noticed one either when visiting the venue or since I'd been here.

"Yes, it's on the next floor up. The views from there are amazing. Come with me, I'll show you."

I followed him out, also ready for some fresh air. We went up in the elevator, but he pressed the button for the tenth floor instead.

"What...?" I started.

"It's the rest of your surprise. The terrace is in our private room. I have a table set out, but that's all I'm telling you. Your parents know about it."

"Oh." I exhaled. He must have set up a candlelit dinner. It was a little crazy to have done it the same night as the party, but I guess he thought he was being romantic.

I followed him into the room. The minute we got inside, before a light was even switched on, I was pushed against the wall, and he smashed his mouth into mine pushing his tongue inside. I tasted scotch, and I knew then he'd been drinking. That was why he'd seemed different. I pushed him away. "Have you been drinking?"

He went into his pocket, and as he did, I switched on the light. It bathed the hotel room in an orange glow, and I noticed right away that there was no balcony and no candlelit dinner.

He held up a silver hipflask. "Care to join me?" Then he shook it. "Oh dear, I appear to have drunk it dry. Never mind, we can get some later." He went over to the bed and patted it. "Come here."

I stood with my hand on my hip. "I don't think so, Julian."

He stood back up, his words slurring. "What? Don't you think you're good enough for me? We have it all planned you know. I'm going to run for senator someday, and I'll need a beautiful wife on my arm. That's going to be you if you play your cards right. Daughter of the great Art and Irena Appleton, with all those contacts. You're perfect. Now get over here and let's seal the deal."

I ran to the door, but he got there before I could open it. "Not so fast, sweetheart. This pussy is mine." His hand went straight to my most private area, and I winced as he cupped me there through my clothes. However, a drunken Julian was no match for my knee, and I turned and kicked him in the balls. While he was crumpled up, I ran from the room. I went straight for the stairs, not waiting on the off chance that he came out of the room and found me before I could escape. I pulled off my sandals and ran down twenty flights of stairs. I didn't want to go back to my party. I didn't want to face my parents, his parents, not even Larissa. How would I explain that I willingly went to a room with him?

I walked as fast as I could out of the hotel, and the doorman instantly got me into a waiting cab. Scrambling for my cell, I opened the message from Parker and gave the cab driver the address. I hoped he had cash on him to pay for my cab because I had none.

I sent a message to my mother saying an emergency had come up and I'd had to leave my party. She quickly responded back with a 'get the hell back here' and 'where was I' but I ignored it. Instead, I texted Parker.

Candy: Please tell me you're there. I'm on my way. I have no money for the cab I'm in.

He replied instantly.

Parker: I'm here. I'll wait at the curb. What happened? I thought it was your party?

Candy: I can't explain right now. I'm just happy you're there.

Next, I sent a text to Larissa saying briefly what had happened and to cover for me, and to tell my mom

I'd booked into a hotel. That I was going to Parker's and I'd be in touch. I slammed my cell into my purse, and with a heavy swallow, I made polite conversation with the cab driver and pretended that my boyfriend hadn't just attacked me, and I wasn't on my way to my teacher's house to fall into his arms in tears.

9

CANDY

Parker walked to the cab driver, paid my fare and then opened my cab door. I went straight into his arms. He lifted me up like I weighed nothing and carried me up a few stairs and into a hallway then through to his apartment. He placed me down on my feet, and I looked around. My eyes took in where he lived—a studio apartment. His double bed was in one corner, a couch in another, a small kitchenette in another. There was an open doorway around which corner I guessed was the bathroom. I'd never thought about where he'd live. It was small, yes. In fact, my bedroom wasn't much smaller than his whole apartment, but it had one amazing thing about it. It had Parker in it.

"Tell me what happened to you." He led me over to the couch, and I sat down.

I told him everything Julian had done.

"I'll kill him."

"No." I shook my head. My cell went off again, and I removed it from my purse, switched it off and placed it back again.

"Do you think that's wise?" Parker asked.

I looked at him. "All my mother is bothered about right now, is the embarrassment that the star guest left her birthday party. Julian was wasted. I have no doubt that in his own clumsy way he was trying to seduce me." I smirked. "His parents talked about us getting married one day. We'd been on one date. A double date. How ridiculous is that?"

Parker's jaw tightened.

"He even said that to me when he tried it on. We should seal the deal." I placed a hand over my mouth. "He was never that into me in the first place, was he? I bet his parents told me I'd make a good trophy wife. He was probably ordered to take me out. I mean someone had to pay for that hotel room, and I don't see how it would have been Julian unless he used his parents' details."

"Do you want a glass of water or anything?" Parker asked.

"Parker." I looked up at him as tears began to fill my eyes. "I want you. Tonight, Julian, he- he could have taken away the one precious thing I have to give. Something I've waited to give to the right man."

"You're a virgin?" he asked, his voice gruff.

I nodded.

"Candy." He stood up and paced slightly. I could see the torment etched into his features, into the edges at the corner of his eyes that crinkled as he thought.

I stood up and reached around and started to lower the zipper on the back of my dress. I then reached a different way as I pulled it down until the dress dropped to my feet in a pool of shimmer. The dress could not be worn with underwear. I was now naked in front of Parker Newell.

His eyes hooded and his gaze darkened. "You looked beautiful tonight in that dress." He paced towards me. "But nowhere near as beautiful as you look now."

His hand went up to my hair, and he unclasped the clip that held half of it back. My hair fell forward over his hand. "If you want me to stop at any time, just say so," he told me. "Because I'm doing this, Candy. I can't stop myself."

He lifted me once more and laid me down on his bed then he moved over the top of me. He was wearing a tee and jeans. I helped him to take off his shirt, pulling it over his head as he lifted his arms. I ran my hands over his body, not believing that we were here. His skin was soft and warm to my touch, but he shivered as I trailed my fingers down his chest, as I felt every muscle. His lips found mine, and he kissed me, softly at first and then with an urgency, a hardness, that I answered with my own fierce kisses. I couldn't wait for him to be inside me. I'd never felt so sure of anything in my life. He moved down lower and took one of my breasts in his mouth, swirling his tongue around it and gently sucking. I could feel it in my core, feel my juices run. He swapped to the other breast and gave it the same attention. Then he trailed his tongue down my stomach. I writhed under his touch. Sometimes it tickled and made me buck more.

Parker positioned himself between my thighs, and I felt his warm breath at the juncture of my pussy. Oh fuck, was he going to lick me *there*? I'd read about it oh so many times, but nothing could have prepared me for when his tongue licked up my slit. I shouted out, "Oh my god," and thrust my hips up to meet his tongue. He raised his head up from my thighs and winked at me. "Do you like that, Candy?"

"Yes," I panted out.

"Do you want me to continue?"

"Parker. Stop talking. Please lick my pussy again," I begged.

With a smirk, his head disappeared back between my legs, but this time he sucked the whole of my clit into his mouth. It felt so, so good. He carried on sucking my clit, licking up my slit and at one point entered my pussy with his tongue. I could feel sensations swirling around my center, and I thrashed against his mouth. Then his tongue went back to my nub, and he flicked it rapidly. Everything focused on that one tiny pleasure point. I erupted over his face, shiver after shiver against his mouth as I rocked. I came down, lying out on the bed as if I'd had fifteen massages in a row. All the tension from what had occurred at my party was gone. Where usually after an orgasm from my own hand I felt shame, now I just craved more. I wanted to feel him inside me. As if reading my mind, Parker moved back up the bed. "Candy, it will feel uncomfortable this time. I'll be gentle, but you need to know that however this feels, there's a reason people love sex. We'll get there, but let's get your cherry popped."

I laughed as he said that and as I did he pushed his cock into me.

I took a large breath as I felt tense.

"Relax around me, baby." He took my hand in his and guided it between our legs. "Feel. I only have the tip in. We're going slow, okay? If you want to stop, just say so."

"I don't want to stop."

"Look right at me, into my eyes as we do this, Candy. Now try to relax."

I looked at him, and all I saw was respect and well,

sheer and utter horniness. Parker wanted me. It was written all over his face.

"You want me," I said out loud.

"So damn much it's almost driven me insane," he replied.

I relaxed, and as I did Parker pushed further into me. I could tell he'd met resistance.

"Here we are, Candy. Ready?"

"Yes."

He pushed further, and I winced a little as I felt a brief amount of pain, and then he slid further inside. There was a feeling then of both pain and pleasure. I felt full. Parker moved slowly, and as the minutes passed, I became accustomed to the new sensations. His pace quickened after a few minutes and then his body tightened before he grunted and I felt a warm gush within me.

He'd come. Parker had cum inside me. We'd done it. I was no longer a virgin. It had been okay, but not like anything I'd ever read about in a book. I knew Parker said it got better but I reminded myself it was fiction I'd read.

"Are you okay?" he asked gently.

"I am." I smiled up at him.

"Oh, Candy. My beautiful, innocent, Candy," he said. "I just made love to you, pretty girl, but when you're recovered and feeling ready for me, I am going to fuck you so damn hard you will see stars."

I gasped. The dirty talk was like in my books, and I felt myself get wet again.

Parker lifted himself from the bed, and I admired his naked ass as he walked toward his bathroom. A few minutes later he returned with a wash cloth, and he wiped between my legs. I saw the cherry red stain that confirmed my virginity was no more. Then Parker gathered me into his arms, "Happy birthday, beautiful woman." I snuggled deeper into him, and we slept for a while.

I awoke to the strangest sensation—pleasure. A finger was between my legs playing with my clit and dipping in and out of my wet pussy. I felt a hard erection pressing into my ass, and I wiggled back against it.

"Good, you're awake. How are you feeling?" Parker asked as he entered me with two fingers.

"I'm fine. Really, fine." I'd expected to be sore, but I wasn't. I was just very, very wet.

Parker continued to play with my clit and dip fingers into my pussy. He brought them up to his mouth and sucked on them. "You taste so good. Later,

I'm going to taste you again, but right now I want to fuck you. Do you want to fuck me right back?"

"I do," I told him.

He moved over me and ran his cock up and down my entrance before positioning himself ready. I brought my hips up toward him, and with how wet I was he began to slide in. I felt him thrust and push into me. There was no barrier now, and with the heat and wetness between my thighs, it felt sensational. I wrapped my legs around him to try to get him deeper inside me. My arms were around his neck, and I dragged my fingernails down his back. I'd read it in a book, and I hoped he didn't hate it. He didn't. Instead, he shivered under my touch and asked me to do it again. "Mark me, Candy, with your nails. Make me yours."

I ran my fingernails down his spine hard, and he thrust into me. I felt so full and looked at where I was. I was full, full of my teacher's cock and I couldn't give a damn. He withdrew from me until only the head of his cock was inside me, and then he thrust back in.

"Oh my god," I shouted.

"You are so fucking sexy, and I'm going to make you scream so hard the other residents of the apartments complain."

He thrust again harder, and the headboard banged the wall. I moaned with the sensations his dick was causing in my pussy. Again and again, he fucked me, the headboard creating its own music against the wall as Parker created a crescendo within me. I could feel myself climbing higher and higher toward my release.

"Harder, Parker, harder," I commanded.

Sweat beaded on his forehead as he gave me his all and as I felt myself begin to climax, I screamed as it erupted. I felt my pussy walls clamp around his cock, my first orgasm during actual sex, and the experience was like nothing I could have imagined. I continued with tiny pulses around him, and even though he'd caused me to come so hard I felt faint, I never wanted his cock to leave my pussy. It belonged there, and I wanted it to feed me orgasms all day and all night. We fucked two more times. The second time he positioned me on top of him, and I rocked up and down on him while he fondled my breasts and kept playing with my clit.

Eventually, entirely exhausted, in the early hours of the morning, I fell back to sleep in his arms, knowing that whatever happened next, I could never regret tonight.

10

CANDY

I woke with a start as I felt someone next to me. Then warm arms gathered me closer, and I remembered where I was and who I was with. Between my legs ached where we'd fucked repeatedly, and I liked it. That word felt so naughty in my mind. We'd fucked. We'd made love, and then we'd fucked—hard. My pussy got damp in reaction to the dirty words in my mind. My fingers strayed down to between my legs. I liked that I could feel Parker had been there. My hand then found his length, and I stroked him, feeling his morning wood. I moved the covers back off us and feeling emboldened I moved further down the bed and took him into my mouth. I seriously had no idea what I was doing. All I knew was what I'd read in books, and so I treated it like a lollipop. I held it at the base and sucked on the end, and then I swirled my tongue around the tip. Parker moved onto his back to give me better access.

I let him go in and out of my mouth while I watched his face. I figured the fact his eyes were shut and his face fixed in concentration meant I was doing okay. I didn't want to just do okay though. I wanted to be the star student of blow jobs! I held him in my hand.

"Parker. Tell me what I can do to make it even better."

He opened his eyes and met my gaze. His stare was lazy, languid. "I'm enjoying what you're doing. Feeling my cock in your warm mouth. Just carry on as you are."

"But help me to make it better," I begged.

"Hold me firmly at the base and pump your hand up and down me as you suck me in and out of that hot little mouth. Then if your mouth aches, do what you've been doing and just swirl your tongue around my glans. You can cup and stroke my balls too. But to be honest, Candy, just the feel of being in your mouth is enough."

"I can't believe I'm here, in your bed," I whispered.

"Me neither. You're like a dream vision. I'm wondering if you're really here or whether I'm still asleep."

"Are you imagining this?" I asked him, and I took him back in my mouth.

I did everything he'd suggested, and after a while,

there was a shift where from being relaxed, Parker had begun to thrust harder into my mouth. His fingers fastened into my hair, and he guided my mouth as his pace quickened. I felt his orgasm begin and then he spurted his cum into my mouth. It tasted salty, and I swallowed it all down, wiping my mouth against the back of my hand.

"Oh my god, Candy," he panted.

After a few minutes, he turned me around and placed himself between my thighs where he teased me into a delicious come of my own with his tongue. By then he was hard once more, and taking care to be more gentle because I was a little sore, he made love to me again.

He showed me his bathroom, and while I took a shower, he made us some scrambled eggs and toast for breakfast along with fresh coffee. Wrapped in a large towel, I sat myself down at his table, and I switched my cell back on.

It beeped with messages.

Larissa: I covered for you. Call me as soon as you can.

Larissa: So much drama went down at your party. Call me asap!

Larissa: Drag yourself away from that man's cock and call me.

Mom: Hope you and Larissa have had a

good time after Julian's behavior. I wished you'd not left the party, but I understand. Let me know when you'll be home. We need to talk.

"I need to call Larissa," I told Parker. He nodded.

"Where have you been? I'm happy your mom didn't call asking to speak to you. Did you do it? Have you been impaled on his cock all night? You are soooo naughty, sexing the teacher."

I laughed.

"I'll catch up with you later. Do you want to meet for coffee this afternoon?"

Parker looked at me and made a sad pout of his lips.

"I have to go home sometime," I whispered. "Plus, you wore it out. It needs to rest."

"I so heard that, you dirty bitch," Larissa squealed, and I flushed. These cell phones were too damn good these days.

"So, tell me, what was the drama?" I asked. "My mom sent me a message that she wants to speak to me. How did my leaving my party go down?"

"Julian came back into the party. He was completely wasted, could hardly stand up. Your mother and his mother went over to him. I'd been talking to your mom at the time, so I followed her. Julian turned to his mother, and he said, no lie, 'Well, it didn't work, Mom. She ran off.' Your mom obviously was concerned as you were missing and asked what he meant and he said, 'I tried to seduce your daughter, but she kneed me in the balls.' Then he turned to his mother and said he was through, that he'd pick his own girlfriends, and to stop pinning their hopes on him and trying to get him to marry well for a future political career because he just wanted to fuck his way around for a while. He was taken out of that party so damn fast. Your mom took out her cell to call for help in finding you and saw your text that you'd left for a while. Then I checked mine and read your message about where you were, and I told your mom I would take you to a hotel for the night and make sure you were okay. Your mom went to find your dad.

Anyway, me and Jeff had the night at the Waldorf, but my mom called me and said your mother gathered everyone and said you'd been the subject of a rather upsetting incident and the party was over. She stopped it and threw everyone out. Mom said she was so classy. But your mom wants to see you as soon as possible. I assured her you were okay and he'd not touched you at all, just got you in the room, because I didn't think you'd want her to know he grabbed you. You need to go home and see them."

I shook my head in agreement though she couldn't see me. "I will. I'll finish my breakfast, and I'll go straight home."

Parker looked at me, concern etched on his face.

"Well, go see your parents and then call me and we'll meet."

"Perhaps it's best I stay home tonight. Why don't you come for a sleepover?"

"Sounds great. As long as you don't think I'm Mr. Newell in the night and try and feel me up."

"I'll call you later," I told her as I ended the call.

"Is everything okay?" Parker asked.

"I need to get home. My parents are really worried."

"I'll drive you," he said. "I'll just grab a quick shower while you finish up your breakfast."

"Thank you. But I might be better off getting a cab."

"I'll drop you off at the end of the street. I'm driving you, and that's final."

"Okay." I stood and wrapped my arms around him and gazed up at him. "I wish we didn't have to hide."

"Well, once you've left school, maybe we won't," he said. "But right now, let's focus on getting you back to your parents, so they can quit worrying about you.

Now, please can we start tutoring again Monday after school because I need to know when I'm going to be able to see you again, just us."

"After school Monday for sure," I told him, reaching on my tiptoes to kiss him.

He groaned. "I'm going in the shower. A very cold shower, or you'll never get home." And he left me to finish up my eggs.

I'd not considered the fact that walking from the end of the road to my house in an almost sheer party dress could have looked like a slutty walk of shame, so instead, I held my head high and acted like I was some kind of celebrity. It was the Upper East Side and barely an eyebrow twitched at my attire.

My mother rushed toward me and enveloped me in her arms. I held myself stiff for a moment before relaxing in her embrace. I didn't think I could remember the last time I'd had a genuine hug from my mother. Not since I was small.

"Come on. Let's go get you changed into something a lot more comfortable and then you can tell me everything that happened."

She ordered refreshments to be sent to my room and sat in one of my velvet chairs in my bedroom while

I went into my closet and changed into pajamas. I hadn't slept well due to being busy with other things, and if Larissa was coming later, I wasn't going to get to sleep until late again. So once I'd spoke to my mom, I was going to try to catch up on some sleep.

I walked back into my room and sat on my bed. My mom poured us both coffee and passed mine to me. She looked me over. "Did that boy harm you in any way? I know you told Larissa he didn't, but I want to hear it from you."

"No, Mom." I saw her visibly relax. "He was too drunk." I described to her how he'd told me he'd arranged a birthday surprise and how foolish I'd felt that I'd entered the hotel room with him.

"But you trusted him. He's a respectable politician's son for goodness' sake. Anyone would have."

"Well, I shouldn't have. Because he was a drunk eighteen-year-old boy and things could have ended so much worse."

"Well, you won't be seeing him again, so that's one less thing to worry about," she said.

"Oh, why's that?" I asked.

"We spoke with his parents early this morning, and Julian is out of Lincoln High, effective immediately. Believe me, they are going to have him very busy out of New York until he proves himself a son worthy of them again."

Now it was my turn to relax. I'd dreaded seeing him again at school.

"I want you to know, Candy, because this came up in conversation last night between your father and me, that we would never expect you to marry for status or money. Obviously, we hope you secure a good future for yourself. But love is more important than money. Your father and I married for love. That's why we're still together after all of these years."

It sounded fantastic until her next sentence.

"Because of course, we have enough money to set you and a husband up in a good home."

I smiled. My mom was who she was. A career woman who had earned her own healthy income, but who was completely at home here in Manhattan among the elite and had no intention of leaving. I doubted she would ever understand if I decided to live differently.

"So, you'd be okay if I went off and married a poor schoolteacher?" I asked.

"Hahahahaha. Oh, Candy. You are so funny. Of course, darling. At least my grandchildren would be well educated." She carried on giggling as she rose to her feet. "I'll let you rest. Thank goodness you're safe. I'm around for the rest of the day if you need me, but tonight, your father and I are at a gala... though I'll cancel if you want me to?"

I shook my head. "I'm fine. Mom. Larissa's coming for a sleepover."

"I can't thank that girl enough for caring for you last night."

"She's amazing," I said honestly.

My mom left the room, stroking my cheek as she left. I felt bad for lying to her, but I couldn't risk her finding out the truth right now. Not until I knew where Parker and I were headed, if anywhere. For now, he was my secret, and it gave an extra frisson to the whole situation. My secret lover. I snuggled down under my comforter and fell asleep to thoughts of the last few hours, the loss of my innocence and how I now really felt like a grown woman.

11

CANDY

My grades meant that I was exempt from finals, and it was the same for Larissa, so we were looking forward to chilling for the last couple months. The gossip was now firmly focused on prom which took place next month. Larissa was beyond excited that she and Jeff were up for King and Queen of senior prom.

Telling Larissa I wasn't sure I'd even go, led to her threatening to not talk to me ever again. "I might be crowned Queen, and you will come and watch me sit on that throne. Plus, Parker will be there chaperoning. I've seen his name on the list."

"You have?"

"Yes, but don't think I'm impressed by the fact that the thought of Parker being there might get you to prom when I couldn't."

I sighed. "Everyone will be there as couples."

"Well, you can third wheel with us, or get a date. I'm sure someone would take Julian's place."

Brandy seated herself at our table. "Replacing him already. That was fast. So, what happened to you at the party? One minute you were there, the next gone, and then Julian disappeared too, and no one could get a hold of him. Something went down... was it you on him?" Everyone around us fell silent, all having wondered what had happened, but none of them having the confidence to ask anything beyond, 'Are you okay?'

"I can't discuss where Julian is, other than I know he's finishing up his education elsewhere. As for me, I had a small accident, but thanks for showing your concern."

She narrowed her eyes. "If it wasn't for you, Julian and I would have been crowned King and Queen of the prom. He was mine first. Then you flirted with him, and he dumped me."

"Hey, Julian asked Candy out. He never even mentioned you. As far as we were concerned, you were an ex," Larissa spat back.

Brandy pushed back in her seat. "This isn't over," she threatened, before stomping away.

"I can't wait to leave this behind. It's worse than kindergarten," I told Larissa.

"And we will," Larissa replied. "After you watch

me be crowned Prom Queen. You do realize she'll score a prom date to try to beat me now, don't you?"

"We'd better get busy with getting you votes then," I told my best friend because there was no way in hell my BFF was losing to that bitch.

I could have groaned when I went to my tutoring —the thing I'd almost combusted over when I'd imagined it—to find Brandy there hanging around Parker with her closest friend Amy. "So, if you'd be in charge of overseeing the coat check team, that would be amazing," I heard Brandy say. God, she was pathetic. She was determined to try to overshadow everyone else on the committee. Her desperation knew no bounds.

As I walked in, she looked at me with a side eye. "Jesus, so impolite, Candy. Have you not heard of knocking? We were in the middle of something." She looked sweetly at Parker, but Parker's attention was on me.

"Well, I have to tutor now, but yes, you can put me down to oversee the coat check. Will I be on a rotation though as I'd like to get to see some of the actual prom."

"Yes, of course. Save me a dance, Mr. Newell," she said. I felt my jaw tighten.

"Come on, Amy," she ordered her sidekick, and they walked out of the room.

When they'd left, Parker raised an eyebrow. "Well,

looks like at prom you'll have to come find me and we'll hide under the coats." He winked.

I sat down. "I wasn't sure if I was gonna go," I told him. "But Larissa said I could go with her and Jeff. That's going to ruin her evening though. It should be romantic for them, not them having me hanging around the whole time."

Parker looked at me. "Hear me out. Now I know you probably don't want to take a date, and I know I don't want to see you with anyone else, but we have to be careful and the best way of handling that right now, is for you to have a date for prom."

My jaw dropped, "But..."

"Think about it. Your parents will wonder why you aren't enjoying the experience, and you said yourself it'll spoil things for Larissa. It's one night, and a date to prom with you might just make some poor boy's night. I know it would have made mine."

"Who did you take to prom?" I asked him.

"I had a girlfriend through high school," he told me cautiously. "We were engaged."

"You were what?" I felt like my world had ended. Here I imagined he was serious about me, when he'd dated and been engaged to someone his own age. I was a fool. I stood to leave, but he grabbed my arm and pulled me toward him, before checking the doorway was clear and keeping me at arms-length.

"It was like Julian. Our parents wanted us together. I didn't love her."

"So you ended it?"

He hesitated.

"Tell me the truth."

"Something happened at my last school. Now, you must believe me. It wasn't true. It was proved not to be true. But Eliza and I split over it anyway. In some ways, the accusation did me a favor."

"What accusation?" I said, but it was like I already knew what he was going to say, and I prayed those words didn't leave his mouth, but they did anyway.

"A student said I'd slept with her. I was investigated."

I swallowed. "You were investigated for having an affair with a student?"

"Yes, but I was innocent," he said. "You have to believe me."

"I'm just one of many, aren't I?" My heart was broken. Tears fell down my cheeks.

I turned to run from the classroom, but his hand snaked out and grabbed my arm. He smashed his lips into mine and steered me to the back of the room. I tried to break away from him, but he was too strong. "No," he said gruffly. At the back of the room, his hands tangled in the back of my hair and he forced my head up.

"Look at me. Please, Candy, look at me."

I did as he asked. Wondering if this was the last time I'd spend with Parker.

"I swear on my life I have never so much as kissed another student. I've dated other women. You should expect that. I'm twenty-four. I have an ex-fiancée. But I can tell you, hand on my heart, that none of them. *None.*" He emphasized the last word. "Have made me feel like you make me feel. I love you, Candy."

"Wh-what?" I said, almost paralyzed by his words.

"I love you, goddamn it. I know it's quick. I know we only just got together, but I can't deny what my heart and body feel. I want you. No one else. Do you believe me? I need you to believe me."

And I did. As literature had taught me, his eyes were the window to his soul, and they told me everything I needed to know. But even if he had been lying I'd have been heading for heartbreak anyhow because I was head over heels in love with Parker Newell and couldn't have walked away if I'd tried.

"Parker."

He looked at me, his eyes downcast and he dropped his hand and stepped back. "I know. I've gone too far. I'll back off, Candy. It'll kill me, but I'll give you space to decide what you want."

"I want you. I love you," I told him.

Then it was like fireworks on the fourth of July as

we came together in an explosion of passion. There was no thought of the fact that anyone could have walked through his door at any time. All the focus went on our tongues tangling, our going short of breath as we kissed each other with a ferocity I would never have believed possible. He backed me against the wall, lifted my skirt around my waist and pulled my panties down my thighs and past my ankles until I kicked them away. I helped him open his zipper until his large, erect cock sprung out to attention and he lined himself up at my entrance and thrust in me, gliding in with ease as I was so damn wet and ready for him.

"Ooooohhhh," I groaned.

He bit the top of my earlobe. "I love it when you make those sounds. They make me want to fuck you harder," he whispered in my ear, and then he thrust into and out of me so hard that I kept slamming into the wall. He lifted my legs, and I wrapped them around him, opening myself up wider so I could accept even more of that impressive dick. It was frenzied, and just a few minutes later I felt Parker tighten as I felt my core quicken. Then I exploded around his cock as he spurted inside me. While I carried on pulsing around his dick he pushed my blouse up and pulling a cup of my bra down, he fastened his mouth on my breast and sucked on it before licking my nipple with his tongue.

Parker came up for air and then it was like we both

realized at the same time where we were and how close we had come to being caught.

"You make me crazy," he told me.

"Take me home," I demanded.

I didn't need to ask him twice, and Larissa covered for me so that I could fuck him twice more in his apartment before returning to my home.

The next day I accepted a prom date from a student called Malachi. He was a nice guy; a little on the quiet side. The fact he wasn't a jock was a winner for me. I explained the date was as friends and he was fine with that. When I told Parker, I saw his face become all jealous which was adorable.

"I want to be your prom date. I know it's impossible, but it's going to be so damn hard seeing you looking beautiful and watching you dancing with other guys."

"Yes, but you get this," I said, grasping hold of his cock on another secret assignation. "They don't."

We were desperate for each other and every moment we got to spend together was treasured.

"When will we be able to be open about us?" I asked him one night after another passionate lovemaking session.

"After graduation?" Parker kissed the top of my head. "I'm going to hand in my notice at the end of the year."

"You are?" I said, stunned. "But what will you do?"

"I have some savings put away until I find something else I want to do. So, for a while, I think I'll just chill with my girlfriend when she's ready to tell her parents about us. That's if they don't kill me, or have me arrested."

It was a worry; I couldn't deny it. I had no idea what my parents' reaction would be to the fact I'd fallen in love with my teacher. However, it was simple. I loved him and if they wanted what was best for me—if what my mother had told me was true, that love was more important than wealth—then we'd be okay. For now, we went on with our forbidden romance, and I prepared myself for prom, where I'd spend the entire evening with someone who wasn't the man I loved, while I posed for pictures pretending I was having the time of my life.

It was typical that a few days before prom I picked up a virus. We were sitting in the cafeteria making last minute plans, and I was almost falling asleep from being up in the early hours being sick.

"Don't you dare not make prom!" Larissa scolded me.

"I'll be there," I said weakly. "If I get some rest tonight and tomorrow, I'll be ready to go Friday for sure."

"Can you believe this room will be turned into an amazing space where we can dance the night away?"

"It's going to be great. I have to say, even though I am loathe to admit it, Brandy has helped coordinate what should be a great prom."

"Yeah, only because she knows she can't win Prom Queen, so she's going for an accolade for best on the committee."

"Well, I didn't think she'd have done it for the good of the school." I smirked.

Larissa looked sad for a moment. "High school's going to be over soon, babe, and then I'm off to Rutger's. I'm gonna miss you."

"Hey, it's only New Jersey. I'll be visiting you and Facetiming you all the time. You can't get rid of me that easily," I reassured her. "Now what should I do with my hair for prom?"

The night of the prom my virus had improved. My gown was amazing and I felt like a princess. The Marchesa number was a floral-embroidered tulle flutter-sleeve gown in light pink. It gave the illusion of a round neckline and pinched in at the waist. It floated all the way to the floor covering my pink satin mule sandals. They had two buckles on them embellished in crystals and were adorable. To finish, I had a lace edged shawl in a jade color.

"Oh my darling, you look stunning. Doesn't she look beautiful, Art?" my mother exclaimed.

"Always, but especially tonight," my dad said.

"Have a lovely time and any hint of trouble from juvenile boys, you tell a teacher, okay? That's why they're there. To keep you safe. Because there's always some boy who'll do a Julian, have too much to drink and try to get fresh with you," my mother added.

I nodded. "I'll be careful." If only she knew it was the teacher who might get fresh with me!

The doorbell rang, and Malachi was escorted into our front room.

"Why, Malachi Hudson, don't you look handsome." My mother embarrassed him with her words, causing his cheeks to flush. He handed me a corsage made up with colors to match my gown, and he had chosen a jade tie to coordinate with the pale green of the leaves on the flowers of my gown and with my shawl.

"Have a good time you two and we'll pick you up at eleven. We want to be there for the final celebration." It was a tradition at our school for the parents to watch the final dance of the night.

My mother embarrassed us further by proceeding to take several photos of us together.

I took Malachi's arm, and he opened the door of the limousine that was taking us back to school. Once I was inside, he closed the door and walked around to the other side, climbing in beside me. Then we were on our way.

"I'm so sorry about my parents," I told him.

"Hey, I didn't think that was too bad. After what happened with Julian, I was expecting my hands to be placed in cuffs for the evening. Hell, I'd have done that if you were my daughter. You look beautiful by the way."

"Thanks," I said. "What do you mean about Julian? I never told anyone what happened."

"I was friends with him." Malachi sighed. "When he left so abruptly I told him he owed me an explanation. Don't worry. I won't tell anyone. He was a dick, and he knows it. For what it's worth he apologized. He's seeing a specialist right now about what happened because his parents felt he was in danger of an alcohol dependency or of attacking another woman if he carried on."

"My parents don't know what he did."

"Well, maybe you should tell them, although I can't see his parents and your parents getting together any time soon. I'm sure your mom would want to know what happened to you."

"I guess." I sighed. "What about his baseball and future political career?"

"Who knows? It's best he gets himself ironed out and takes it from there."

"Thanks for telling me what's happening with him, and for respecting I want to keep things private."

"No problem," he said. "Now please tell me we're going to dance the night away and make this the best prom ever."

I high-fived him. "You betcha."

We walked into the school and straight to the cloakroom. My heart caught in my chest as I saw Parker. He was dressed in a black and white tux and looked oh so handsome. He was busy helping others check in jackets and shawls. I handed him my shawl and he'd still not noticed I was there until I spoke. "If you could hold this for me until later," I requested. He stopped suddenly and looked up at me.

"Miss. Appleton. You look very lovely this evening, and Mr. Hudson, you, my man, look very smart. He touched my hand, stroking it as he moved the shawl away from me. "Have a great time, you two."

"Thanks," I replied, and I walked away, adding an extra shimmy to my step on his behalf.

As we walked into the decorated cafeteria, there

was a photo area where Malachi and I posed for the customary official photos. Everyone exclaimed over each other's outfits. It was so strange because we were celebrating the end of school, and our new career paths and future lives. It was kinda happy and sad at the same time. I'd spent years with some of these people, and after high school, I might never see them again.

We walked to the dance floor and danced the night away, only stopping for quick refreshment breaks. Then it was time to announce the Prom King and Queen and our evening was made when Larissa and Jeff were crowned. Larissa squealed so high, I was surprised all the glass in the building hadn't shattered. They walked on the stage and sat in the specially created thrones and then last year's Prom King and Queen had crowned them both.

Despite the fact I wasn't able to spend the evening with my true love, I'd had the most amazing time.

"Hey, Candy," Malachi whispered in my ear. "Would you mind if I had a couple of dances with Shannon?" I turned and looked at the willowy brunette hovering nearby. I recognized a potential hook-up when I saw one. I leaned over and kissed his cheek. "Thanks for everything. The night has been amazing, but you go and spend the last part of the evening with Shannon. Our parents will be here soon to suck the joy out of the end of the celebration."

Malachi laughed, and after giving me a hug, he went off with Shannon.

I looked around. I figured there couldn't be a need for too many people in the coat check right now. I took out my phone and sent a text to Parker.

Candy: Your classroom in 5?

A few seconds later my phone beeped.

Parker: I'm on my way.

I pushed open the classroom door, and then I locked it behind me. The moonlight lit up his features, and he looked like some movie star to me. I walked up to him, and he ran a hand down my face.

"You look so beautiful tonight."

"You look so handsome."

"You look far too beautiful for me to touch. I shouldn't risk messing up your appearance."

"I dressed for you."

He took his cell from his pocket and pressed some keys until Ed Sheeran's *Thinking out Loud* sang out from the speaker. Then he gathered me into his arms.

"If we can't dance together in public, then we'll do it here in private."

And so we did. We slow danced through the whole of the song, and then he kissed me. And then once again we couldn't help ourselves. He carefully removed my dress until I stood in front of him in just a silver lacy bra and thong. He removed his pants and boxers, and then he bent me over a desk at the back of the room. My hands grasped onto the edge as he pushed my thighs apart with his knee. He brought a hand beneath my legs and pushed the thong to one side.

"So, so, wet. Is that all for me?"

"Yes, you. Only you." I gasped.

His fingers played me like a musical instrument. I was putty in his hands. Almost insane with need I wiggled my ass back and ground into his erection.

"Fuck me, please."

He teased my wet slit with the tip of his cock. "Maybe I'll just tease you like this? Just teasing your wetness and pinching your clit." He pinched me with the fingers of the hand not holding his cock, and I gasped.

"No, please. I need you. I want to feel you deep inside me."

He thrust into me with no warning then, so I screamed in ecstasy. I was so full of his cock, and it was glorious. This was where I belonged—with Parker. I couldn't get enough of him. If he fucked me all day and all night, it would never be enough. We craved each other, and I knew I needed this man to be mine forever.

Just as I felt my come approaching, Parker withdrew. Turning me around, he lifted my ass and deposited me onto the edge of the top of the desk before ramming his cock back into me.

"Marry me, Candy." He groaned.

"What?" I thought my ears were tricking me.

He stopped thrusting. "I realize there are more romantic ways to propose, but I can't wait. I need to know now. Will you marry me, Candy? I don't care where. I don't care when. Just say you'll be my wife?"

"Yes. Oh my god, Parker, yes."

He thrust back inside me, and we headed toward our completion, too wrapped up in each other to realize that someone had unlocked the door.

Until the principal's voice yelled. "What the hell is going on here?"

12

PARKER

What had I done?

I certainly wasn't going to be awarded 'Teacher of the Year' at prom.

Or, 'Boyfriend of the Year' by my lover's parents.

I'd seduced my student in the classroom and been caught by the principal, and I'd proposed mid-sex.

I deserved everything I got.

Principal Lancaster had given us a few minutes to get dressed and was waiting for us in her office.

Candy was in tears.

The shock had made her sick. She'd run out of the classroom once dressed and straight into the restroom.

It was only a matter of time before the principal called her parents and that's if they weren't already here. We were near the end of the night and the last dance. This was not how any of this was supposed to go down.

I pushed the door of the girl's restroom open. Hell, I was done anyway, so what did it matter?

I found Candy cornered in there by another student, Brandy Elliott.

"You made me look like an idiot and cost me the Prom Queen title. Now how do you think your last days here are gonna go down? You're just a slut. Julian will be able to come back now because your reputation will be destroyed."

"Get out," I shouted at Brandy.

The student turned to me and laughed. "I'm going, but that's because I'm done here. I don't have to listen to you. I doubt very much you're a teacher here anymore. I'm off to let the rest of the prom know what I heard at the door. Too busy fucking to realize how loud you were. You're disgusting, the pair of you." With that, she waltzed out of the door.

Candy collapsed into my arms.

"Parker, what will we do?"

"I'll tell you what we're going to do," I said, and then I helped her clean up.

We walked into the cafeteria, and everyone's gazes fell on us. You could see the shock and hear the whispers. One of the teachers came up to me and told me I should leave the room and that Principal Lancaster was waiting.

"She can wait a few more minutes," I told him. "I'm dancing with my girl at her prom."

And we did. We walked into the center of the dance floor and started dancing. I wrapped my arms around her tight. After a few seconds, others began to dance around us. When the song finished, I walked Candy over to the photo area and asked the photographer to take our photo.

"Now, we'll leave," I said to the staff standing by, no doubt ready to escort me from the room if necessary, and we went to see the principal.

I handed in my resignation, effective immediately, and asked that Candy not be punished, that she be allowed to graduate, and that I would stay away from the graduation ceremony. I didn't want to, but for Candy and her family's sake, I needed to.

My resignation was accepted, but Principal Lancaster warned me that Candy's family might want to take legal action against me.

Then there was a knock at the door, and it opened, revealing Candy's parents.

"What the hell is going on here?" her father asked.

"I'd like to explain." I stood up.

I should have anticipated the punch before it came and the blow hit me straight in the jaw.

We left the venue and went to Candy's home where she explained that we'd been in a relationship since after her eighteenth birthday. To say her parents were shocked was an understatement. I listened as Candy explained that what she had said happened with Julian that night hadn't been the whole truth and that shortly afterward we had started a relationship. I noticed she kept up the fabrication that Larissa had stayed with her after the events with Julian, and realized that she was determined to protect her best friend.

"I'm finding it hard to process all this," her mother said.

"I love your daughter," I told them both. "I'll look after her with every bone in my body for the rest of her life. I wouldn't treat her like Julian did. I proposed to Candy tonight. She had agreed to marry me."

"What?" her father almost choked. "We have standards in this house to adhere to, and so far, Parker, you have shown no respect for any of them. Get out of our house," he roared.

"Mr. Appleton, I—"

"*Get out* before I hit you again," he warned.

Candy looked up at me, and I saw the resignation in her eyes. She wanted me to leave. Whether it was just for tonight or for forever, I didn't know.

I stood up and picked up my jacket.

"I'm at my apartment if you need me," I told her, and she nodded.

And then I left her house, returning to my apartment with no job and the possibility I'd lost the love of my life as well on the same night.

13

CANDY

I had spent the next few days lying around in my room like I was sick. I had still felt off anyway. Embarrassed, I refused to go to school on Monday. I'd heard nothing from Parker, despite repeatedly checking my cell. I wondered what I'd expected to happen. He'd told me where he was if I needed him. Was I expecting text after text? Larissa had called, but I'd made a big deal out of still feeling sick because as sympathetic as she was, she was still high on being the Prom Queen, and Jeff had suggested setting a wedding date later that same night. I could hardly tell her Parker had proposed to me; that would have been stealing my girl's thunder. Anyway, as I'd said, it was true anyway. I felt weary like all I wanted to do was sleep. I had no appetite either. Everything made me feel nauseous. I was love sick.

My mother had kept checking on me, but had mostly left me alone. That was all about to change though as I woke from a nap to find her sitting in one of my purple velvet chairs.

"It's time for us to talk about the future, darling."

"Oh, Mom." I groaned. "I don't want to."

"You can't pretend none of this has happened, Candy, and you need to make some decisions. You have a man going demented wondering whether or not you still want him."

I turned to her. "What do you mean?"

"Parker has called here several times a day but asked me not to tell you. He said he wanted you to make up your own mind with no influence from him. But I can't sit here watching you check out of life, pining for him when he's doing the same over you."

I sat up. "He is?"

"Yes. Candy…" My mom paused. "Do you really love him? Do you see a future with him?"

I started to answer, but she held up a hand.

"With no pressure or influence from him, sweetheart, just from your own heart. We can be on a plane out of here this afternoon and go to a spa until you feel ready to face the world again."

"I love him so much my heart is breaking," I confessed, and I started to sob.

My mom got to her feet. "Then get in that shower.

Get yourself washed and breakfasted and then go and tell him that."

"What about Dad?" I asked.

"I've spoken to your father. He's better, or rather he's coming around to the fact his little girl is not a little girl anymore. Just promise me one thing. That Parker did not start anything with you while you were underage."

"I swear on my life, Mom, he didn't, and I pursued him, Mom. I love him so much." I swung my legs out of bed and went dizzy, reaching for the edge of the bed to steady myself.

"You're still not well are you?" my mother noted. "Stay there while I go to get you something to eat."

She returned fifteen minutes later with a tray, but there wasn't only orange juice and a croissant on it. There was also a pregnancy test kit.

"I think you ought to do that," she told me. "To be certain as to whether or not you truly have a virus, as I'm not so sure."

Reassured by the test, having enjoyed my breakfast and showered, and now feeling fresh, I got in my car and drove to Parker's apartment.

I rang the doorbell and waited.

The man who answered the door made my heart sink, and I wanted to cry. He was unshaven. Dark shadows looked like bruises underneath his bloodshot eyes.

"Candy!" he exclaimed. "You're here, you're really here. Come in."

"I need to talk to you," I told him, and I walked past him and sat down on his couch.

"Oh," he said, his head bowed, and he pulled up a dining chair to sit across from me. "Come on," he said. "Just say it. We're breaking up, right?"

"We're pregnant," I told him.

I thought he was going to fall off his seat.

"We're what?"

"We're pregnant. I have no idea how far along I am. I just did a test like an hour ago. And then another two because I couldn't believe the results. But, yes, we're pregnant."

"And how do you feel about that?" Parker asked me tentatively.

"Well, let me see. I have the most handsome and sexy fiancé in the whole world, and now I'm having his baby. I think I feel pretty damn fantastic." I smiled. "Apart from occasionally feeling like I have the flu."

He launched at me from his seat, crushing his mouth to mine, but being careful not to crush me. "I thought I'd lost you. I love you, Candy Appleton." He sat back and placed a hand on my stomach. "And you, little one."

I started to laugh.

"Could you please take a shower and shave, your stubble is giving my face an itchy rash," I told him.

"Yes. I'll be right back." He leapt from the room and straight into the shower. And then we spent the next few hours making up for lost time.

EPILOGUE
CANDY

I attended my graduation. It was a lovely way to say goodbye to my high school days. The ring on my finger shut down any gossip that Brandy had tried to fire my way. Everyone was bored with her drama by now. We'd all grown up, and she needed to do the same.

Saying goodbye to Larissa as she headed off to University with Jeff was heartbreaking, but we'd had an amazing time when she'd been my bridesmaid.

Parker had visited my father, alone, and following that had re-proposed to me in the middle of Central Park on a carriage ride. He'd placed on my ring finger a spectacular ring from Tiffany's with a large center diamond surrounded by a double row of bead-set diamonds. I had no idea how he had afforded it and hoped my parents hadn't given him the money. I didn't want to start our married life with misconceptions that I needed to be surrounded by wealth, and I'd told him so.

Which was when he'd confessed that he was the heir to a huge publishing company. I was shocked. He'd told my parents when he'd visited to ask my father for my hand in marriage, but as my mother had apparently told him, just as she had me, it was love that counted to her, not money. Of course, later in conversation with me, true to form, she'd said she was damn happy he was loaded though and that I wouldn't have to strive for anything in my life. She'd never change, but she was my mom, and I loved her.

When we'd told my father I was expecting a baby, I seriously thought we were going to have to call 911. My mom later told me that realizing his baby was growing up was enough of a shock. To find out that his baby was having a baby had almost caused a coronary.

We had an elaborate wedding held at the Waldorf. It was what we wanted. We wanted to show the elite of Manhattan that we'd done nothing to be ashamed of and I wanted my fairy tale. I had my prince, and I wanted to be a princess for a day. Everything I had read about in my romance novels was becoming part of my real life.

"You're daydreaming again," my husband's voice whispered next to my ear. "I swear you spend as much time in your imaginary world as you do in the real one."

I smiled at him. "Well, I do have a novel to write."

"Yes, and can you hurry, because I know the team are waiting to read it."

I laughed. Parker had gone to work at the family firm and found out he enjoyed working there. He said he had been as obstinate as his father and had refused to work there because his father told him he had to. Once we had a baby on the way, he'd lost his stubbornness. We had submitted my first novel to them blind. They'd offered me a two-book deal, and now they were waiting for the second book. Parker had also helped to set up a reading charity after I'd told him my dream to help people less fortunate.

My days were spent in our home in Manhattan, between writing words in a fictional world and living the dream of real life with my handsome husband and our beautiful daughter, Posey.

Parker licked the tip of my ear. "Have you been writing any sexy scenes in there lately?" He nodded toward the manuscript.

"Maybe..." I teased.

"Well, I think we should go try them out, you

know, to check for authenticity. I wouldn't want you to write something that wasn't doable in real life."

"What about our daughter?" I asked him.

"Fast asleep in her bed," he said smugly. "Daddy has the magic touch."

"Anyway," he added. "You promised me we'd have babies every couple years and she's fifteen months old now, so we need to start making the next."

"I did, didn't I?" I saved my file and closed my laptop. "Well, it just so happens that I need to write a scene where the woman sits right on a hot man's cock on a seat in the middle of her vast library, surrounded by books."

"Hmmm, I think my wife is lying as this has already happened in real life many, many times." Parker nibbled my neck.

"I'm writing it in this novel because it's my favorite scene. It should be immortalized in ink forever."

"Well, after that, later tonight, can we play naughty teacher, because that is my best fantasy come to life."

"Yes, Sir," I answered, and with a groan, he lifted me off my feet and ran with me into the house.

THE END
Want more forbidden student romance?

TRY FEMALE PROFESSOR/MALE STUDENT
TEACH HER.

Read on for a sneak peek...

TEACH HER
CHAPTER ONE

Meredith

Being a professor got real stressful at times and that was why sometimes, if we stayed late preparing lesson plans or marking, myself and Marcus Wilson would give each other a helping hand to release some of the tension. We weren't fuck buddies—it had never gone that far—we were come buddies.

It had begun the middle of last year. A day that had been extraordinarily hot, and I had had fractious and short-tempered students being smart asses the whole day. It was a problem I expected to address only at the beginning of a semester. The grad students were at least eighteen years old, and at twenty-five I wasn't *that* much their senior. But senior I was, and I had made sure they had learned that pretty damn quick. For the most part students were respectful, but you always had the odd one who had had a bad day or was struggling with life at that particular time. The day we became come buddies, a student had walked out of class after giving me a heap of abuse and I was still new to that kinda confrontation. The stress, added to a shitload of work I had to finish and prepare, meant I had ended up in my office determined that I was not getting behind the wheel until I had calmed myself the fuck down. Marcus had also stayed late and popped in to my office to see me, before he left. We had gotten along pretty well from the get-go and maybe I would have dated him if either I had a) wanted a relationship, or b) it hadn't been against the school's policies. He was cute in an Orlando Bloom kind of way: sexy, but with a young and fresh face, freckles, and a smile that quirked the corner of his lip.

"You look like you need vodka," he'd told me, taking a hip flask from his laptop bag and handing it over.

"That transparent, huh?" I'd replied. "I've been in here for two hours now, trying to get caught up on things and attempting to calm myself down."

He'd lightly stroked my forearm. "I heard about the face-off with Fleishman."

A heavy sigh had left my mouth. "I'm trying to forget about it."

He beckoned me upright and put an arm around me. "Come here. Let Prof. Wilson give you one of his amazing hugs."

Despite the heat, I'd snuggled up into his arms. It had been exactly what I'd needed. Just to know that someone else gave a damn that my day had been the pits. However, after a few minutes it was clear that we were both too hot.

"Thanks, but I am going to pass out if I stay next to your shirt any longer." I smiled.

"Well, I could always take it off?" he'd said.

"I don't want a relationship."

"Neither do I. Why don't we just give each other a helping hand... or tongue." He'd winked. "Get rid of some of that stress."

The day had sucked and so I'd thought fuck it. I'd not dated anyone for over a year due to a bad break up and the thought of enjoying myself with no baggage had sounded fine to me.

So that's when it had started—*the helping hand.*

We'd ended up back here today. Back in my office on the very last day of term. Marcus was leaving. Everyone had gone, and it was just the two of us.

"So, what do you think?" he said to me, "Go big, or go home?"

I unbuttoned my blouse, revealing the white lacy bra I wore underneath.

"Well, it's you, so I would say it's most definitely go big."

Marcus had a nine-inch cock. It was larger than any cock I'd ever seen before. I'd become practiced in the art of jacking him off with my hands and my mouth, but today—our very last time together—we were going for the grand finale, and I couldn't wait. It had been so long since I'd ridden any cock, never mind one that I fully expected to give me a good time. Plus, the thought of someone walking in on us since we'd started doing this, made my juices flow. Now we were going to fuck, I was in danger of flooding the school.

Marcus stripped out of all his clothes and then grabbed me and pushed me over to the wall. Kneeling at my feet, he pulled my thong down my thighs, calves, and off, leaving them bunched at the side of him, then he moved my thighs apart. My pussy was swollen and ready to accept the tongue that knew exactly how to bring me off. His mouth fastened on my bud sucking eagerly and he pushed two fingers inside my soaking wet heat.

"Oh my god. Yes."

Within a minute I had to hold his head with my hands as I tried to push my core closer to his mouth. My cream dripped down his face as I exploded against his lips.

We paused for a moment as he allowed me the time to recover from my shudders.

Changing position, I took him in my mouth. I was still so horny my juices ran down my legs and dripped onto the floor. Marcus groaned as I sucked him right to the back of my throat, but because this time things were to end differently, I kept stopping when I felt him get too eager, so he didn't come in my mouth.

"Ready?" he asked me.

"Yes."

He unwrapped a condom and placed it on his cock and then he lined himself up with my entrance, pushing in deep. I could feel his girth slowly sinking inside my walls, filling me up inch by glorious inch and I couldn't help but make noises. I loved to talk dirty too.

"Oh fuck. Why didn't we do this sooner? Oh my, your cock is so huge. It's filling me right up."

Marcus' hands gripped my hips harder. He didn't

speak. Instead, he showed me with his actions that he was enjoying himself.

As I began to raise my hips to meet his thrusts, he moved his hands around to my breasts, leaning down to capture a nipple in his mouth which he then sucked on.

"Ooooooohhhh."

I felt myself building towards completion once more. Marcus abandoned my nipple as he concentrated more on the rhythm of his thrusts. Though he quickened his pace, he remained quite gentle though and to be honest I wanted him to fuck me hard, so I told him so.

He thrust a little harder, but I could tell it wasn't his thing and he returned to giving me a slow and steady fucking. I needed more and so while he thrust inside me, I reached down and played with my own clit until I felt the tremors of my come begin. I quivered around his cock, milking it as he reached his own climax with an, "Oh God," of his own. He pulled me in close to him and we stayed there, joined together, bodies close until we got our breath back. Then he looked up at me.

"Goodbye, Prof. Butler. It's been a pleasure."

"It certainly has." I peeled myself away from his body and I picked up my panties. "What am I going to do for stress relief now?" I laughed, as we cleaned ourselves up with our discarded underwear.

"Looks like you'll have to discover wine."

He knew I didn't drink much though he didn't know why.

"Maybe."

"It's a shame I'm moving so far away," he said. "We could still have met up."

"I'll have to bring a battery-operated boyfriend with me to school along with my laptop." I winked. "And seeing as I have one that looks exactly like a lipstick, I'll have to make sure not to reapply in front of the students, just in case I take out the wrong one."

He laughed. "So, what are you doing over the break then? You know I'm relocating. What are your plans?"

"I'm going to hit the gym hard," I said. "I've wimped out so many times after classes because of being exhausted. It's time to get my fitness back up to its prior levels. Other than that, not a lot. I intend to visit my family for as short a time as I can get away with and hit the beach to get a golden glow."

He leaned over and kissed my cheek.

"No. We can't leave it like that," I told him and I placed my hands at the back of his head and brought his lips to mine. We had never kissed on the mouth. Intimate kisses of private areas but never our mouths. The kiss was long, tender, and a proper goodbye.

He left. I watched him go and then I sat back on my chair for a while, so that we didn't leave together. It was something Marcus had always insisted on. I didn't give a damn if the janitor saw us walk out together. They could assume what they liked, there was no proof. We kept the door locked. Next semester wouldn't be the same.

Try as I might though, I couldn't conjure up any real feelings for Marcus. He really had been a means to an end. Like a real-life dildo. I felt guilty about my feelings, but it was for the best that while I had enjoyed our make-outs, I had developed nothing in the way of a crush and had never wanted to take it further. He was now gone and my sex life had left with him, but if I missed anything, it would be our friendship.

The break passed, and I had indeed gotten myself back to the gym. My body had toned enough that I felt happy wearing my tiniest gym shorts and a crop top. My arms and thighs were well defined now, and my abs had a six pack I was immensely proud of. I made a promise to myself that no matter how stressful school got when I returned, I would maintain a fitness regime to keep myself toned. Maybe I wouldn't be able to maintain the athletic figure I had right now, but I felt so much better in myself when I was fitter, and so the gym and the pool needed to become part of my own curriculum. I was so busy daydreaming, I stumbled on the treadmill and felt myself falling, only to be caught by a well-toned pair of arms.

"Fuck. Thanks so much," I told the owner of them as I rubbed the back of my neck. "I let my concentration go. Stupid of me. I think that's a sign I need to stop and get some water."

"Stand there. I'll get you a drink," the guy said, and I watched as he walked away.

He was of medium build, around six feet tall, and had almost jet-black hair that was a little grown out. I guessed you'd call it shaggy. His eyes had been the most piercing blue, and chiseled cheekbones and a full pout made him look like some kind of model. I guessed that's exactly what he was, plenty of models frequented my gym. They sold photos to independent authors to use as their cover pictures on books; and our gym owner, Macy, an obsessive reader, liked to frame the covers and put them up on walls around the gym. Hell, I had no objections! It was better than staring at my own sweaty body while I exercised. I'd chatted to a few of the models at times. Some were lovely and down to earth, while others thought they were God's gift to men and women, but I'd never seen this guy before so I presumed he was a new one.

He walked back over and held out the drink to me. I stared at him a little more while trying not to be too obvious about it.

"Thanks," I said as I reached for the paper cup of water. I drank it down greedily.

"Nice tat," he said to me when I'd finished and could speak again. He nodded toward my upper hip. Visible above my gym shorts was a tattoo of an egg timer, the sand was part pouring out. The timer was black and the sand purple and aqua blue. It was only small, but I'd had it done at the beginning of the summer break to remind me that life carried on whether I was being present in my life or not. I'd done a lot of thinking and looking inward during vacation time and had vowed to open myself up to new opportunities. I'd been scared to get into another relationship, having found the heartbreak of before so soul destroying, but Marcus had helped me see that I wanted more. Maybe not a relationship still—I remained cautious after my break-up with Chad—but I wanted my heart to thump faster and I liked things on the dirtier side of the spectrum. I'd wanted Marcus to pound me hard on our onetime fuck. As a full-on lover, he wouldn't have been enough. I also liked the danger that we could have been caught. I wondered how people found lovers who could give them what they wanted and whether it just came from a relationship developing over time. My big break-up relationship had contained perfectly adequate sex, but we were both new to relationships. Chad and I had met at high school and neither of us had been confident enough to ask for what we wanted. Still, I'd loved Chad, and it had killed me inside when we'd broken up after six years together.

"Perhaps I would have been better grabbing you an espresso?" the guy stated, and I realized I had completely zoned out on him.

"Jeez, I'm so sorry. I really don't feel quite myself today." I looked down at my tat. "It's there to remind me that life is short and to enjoy myself," I explained.

"I wholeheartedly agree," he replied. "But today I think you should call it a day and head home and grab some sleep. Start the whole 'making the most of life' mantra tomorrow."

I laughed. "Yes, you're right. I'm going to get showered under very cold water, grab a coffee—though I'll make it a latte rather than espresso—and then I'm gonna head on home to sunbathe on the deck in the shade, where I may just fall asleep. Thank you once again for coming to my rescue." I held up my empty paper cup. "And for the water."

"No problem," he replied. Those blue eyes twinkled when he smiled and revealed perfect, white teeth. He held out a hand. "Garrett."

"I'm Meredith." I decided to brazen it out. "Are you one of the cover models?"

He shook his head and laughed. "No. I'm nothing special. Just here to make the most of what God gave me and keep it healthy, you know?"

"Totally. My summer has been devoted to it. Well, that and catching up on trash TV, but I don't usually admit to that. Anyway, enough of my chatting. I ramble on when I first meet someone, I think it's nerves. See you around." I said, and then I left, moving as quickly as I could. I felt rather stupid that I'd asked if he was a model now. He probably thought I was some kind of groupie, jeez. That would not do. I would have to work on potential topics of conversation that didn't make me out to be some complete brainless airhead. What was it I had said? That I wanted to catch up on reality TV. Dear God. The guy had looked a little younger than me and yet he had seemed so much more mature in the confidence that had oozed from him and how he had handled himself. I seriously could do with some pointers. Maybe for now though I would just change the time I went to the gym slightly, so I could avoid embarrassing myself again for the last week of the break.

CARRY ON READING: **TEACH HER**

FREE STORY WITH NEWSLETTER SIGN UP

Did you know I have a newsletter? I love it because I can write to you with news of work-in-progress, sales, giveaways, and general updates about my life!
You also get a FREE short story, the prequel to Rats of Richstone, BAD BAD BEGINNINGS.
So sign up today. I look forward to connecting with you.
Angel xo

https://geni.us/angeldevlinnewsletter

ABOUT ANGEL

Angel Devlin writes stories about bad boys and billionaires. The hotter, the better.
She lives in Sheffield with her partner, son, and a gorgeous whippet called Bella.

When not working, she can be found either in the garden, drinking coffee, watching too much TikTok, or daydreaming about her ideal country cottage.

She's a firm believer in living in, and enjoying every moment and hopes her words bring you that enjoyment. Let her know by leaving a review, joining her newsletter, or dropping her a line via Facebook DM or email.

E-mail: contact@angeldevlinwriter.com

THE FORBIDDEN FANTASIES SERIES

RULE HIM
Male teacher/Female student romance

TEACH HER
Female professor/Male student romance

More titles to come.

Printed in Great Britain
by Amazon